What's Lc

"Life is what you make of it, the way you take it; good, bad or blessed." These words from their beloved sister-in-law Olivia echo in the hearts of the McConnell sisters—Dora, Kat, and Pearl—two years after her passing.

Pearl travels the world as an acclaimed photographer, while Kat owns the successful Café By The Seaside restaurant chain spanning the Texas coast and two Hawaiian Islands. Both sisters are using their work and travel to move forward and want their sister Dora to do the same.

Dora has built a peaceful life as a seashell hunter and souvenir shop owner, but still quietly grieving Olivia's loss... her world is upended when a new neighbor, Harper "Hawk" Harrison, moves in next door to her beach house on the family ranch.

Hawk has only himself to worry about and a drive to see new places and buy and renovate homes everywhere. He has a fantastic eye that sees what a place could be and brings it to its best. When he meets Dora, in his mind nothing needs to change, yet he senses somewhere deep inside she has a secret.

As life on Star Gazer Island takes unexpected turns, Dora finds herself drawn to more than just her beloved seashell creations and moonlit walks by the topaz waters. Her carefully guarded heart begins to stir with new possibilities, promising adventures she never imagined when she realizes sitting on that rock alone in the moonlight is better with Hawk beside her. But can she risk loving and maybe losing?

Life on Star Gazer Island is about to shine as brilliantly as wet seashells under a midnight moon, as the sisters discover that moving forward from loss can lead to unexpected joy.

WHAT'S LOVE GOT TO DO WITH IT

Sun Over Star Gazer Island, Book One

DEBRA CLOPTON

What's Love Got To Do With It
Copyright © 2025 Debra Clopton Parks

This book is a work of fiction. Names and characters are of the author's imagination or are used fictitiously. Any resemblance to an actual person, living or dead, is entirely coincidental.

All rights reserved. No part of this publication may be reproduced, distributed or transmitted in any form or by any means, including photocopying, recording, or other electronic or mechanical methods, without the prior written permission of the publisher, except in the case of brief quotations embodied in critical reviews and certain other noncommercial uses permitted by copyright law. For permission requests, please contact the author through her website: www.debraclopton.com

CHAPTER ONE

Wearing her well-worn morning seashell hunting shorts, T-shirt, and flip-flops, Dora McConnell walked down the back steps of her cozy seaside home and headed toward the blue waters and her beach.

Her private cove that joined the large bay along the Corpus Christi coast, but this was her place, her secluded beach.

Feeling no need to be too close to anyone, she loved this spot on their huge family ranch because it was on the edge of their property and so near the beach. For her, walking on the beach was one of her most cherished and inspiring places to be. Especially since she created seashell art for her store and loved every moment of creating.

This morning her heart was hurting as it had been for the last two and a half years since losing her brother's first wife, her best friend. She loved Matt's new wife, Kelley, who had lived through a past of sorrow and trauma herself, as had so many people in this world. Dora reminded herself often of this fact but still, she missed sweet Olivia. She was thankful that Matt had found Kelley and knew Olivia was too.

Kelley built homes with beautiful glass portions in the roofs and walls to help most people see the beauty surrounding them. For Kelley, a builder who had lost her father, when he had died saving Kelley by throwing her out of the way when the house caved in. The trauma left Kelley dealing with fear and deep grief. Dora's brother had helped Kelley overcome her fears and they fell in love during that time. They now lived here on the coast in an amazing home Kelley had designed with glass ceilings and walls that overlooked the ocean. And from the beams hung a beautiful, colorful glass ornament that sparkled the living space up as the sun shown through the glass at certain times of the day. They'd bought it at a special Christmas auction because they'd heard from friends how amazing it was going to be. Her brother wanted it for his and his wife's new home as a sparkling reminder of love; his lost love and new-found love.

WHAT'S LOVE GOT TO DO WITH IT

When he and Kelley had seen the ornament up close they'd known it was perfect for them. Thus, they'd won the auction and the large price tag had gone to support the shelter for women, No Place Like Home in Mule Hollow, Texas. It was a blessing to all involved, just like the talented ornament creator often used her auctions for. And now, the ornament hung from the ceiling of her brother's home, and now in the sunlight it sent sparkles of colored light dancing through the room and brought a smile to everyone's face.

Olivia's beautiful smile had done the same.

Now, as Dora stared out across the ocean as the early morning waves washed in over her bare feet, she smiled at the blessing of a new day. This was what gave her happiness, searching for seashells to use in her store to bring smiles to her customer's faces. She placed reasonably priced items for all the tourists who came inside. Making sure that there was something anyone could buy to take home as a memory of visiting Star Gazer Island. Her island was a jewel all of its own.

Now, restless she took a breath, her brain was rolling with the waves this morning. Lately, Dora felt this way more than ever. Which for her as everyone would say was unusual. She was the calm one. The loner. The easy going shell seeker.

Olivia took joy out of every moment of life and it

had been stunning to watch her determined to make people smile and she enjoyed every second she had on earth before she stepped into heaven. Her brother had been so strong during that time then he'd taken off, hit the road for two years. He'd taken Olivia in his heart on the trips they'd talked about as a distraction from the pain Olivia was feeling before she died. After being away from all of them and unable to move back home, he'd gone to their old home place, met Kelley and fallen in love again.

Exactly what Olivia had wanted for him. Dora was torn thinking about it.

Was that what was pinching her—that Olivia had wanted her to experience love? Live life fully and not let it pass her by? She loved her life, her quiet life. Her protected life here in her cove. What if she took that chance at love then had to live through losing the man she took that chance with? She couldn't do it, there were reasons. She was a wimp and finding love and losing it was something she never wanted to experience. But this morning as waves washed in around her feet, curling up around her ankles before sliding away and back out to the sea, she felt Dora urging her forward like never before. Her heart hurt.

She sighed and turned, no seashell hunting today. It was time to get to her shop, get her thoughts on people coming in so that she could make them smile. But, as she headed back toward her house the thought hung over her, she couldn't keep living and thinking like this forever.

She walked to the water spout next to her steps and washed her feet off before heading into her home. Inside she scanned the room, this was home. Her comfortable, small but open area with her amazing view of the ocean through the large glass doors. She was blessed. She loved her life.

Her mind back on target, she put the thoughts to rest. If she was supposed to fall in love like Olivia had wanted her to do, she would. So wandering around restless like today was ridiculous. She shoved her hand through her thick, golden hair as she walked to her bathroom and turned on the shower. It was time to get back to work. It was time to get over being lonely.

Lonely was the right word. She pushed it away; she had a life, and lacking a special man didn't mean it wasn't a fulfilled life. It was time to dress, open her store, before meeting her sisters for dinner. It was a very special dinner she was looking forward to. So, she dressed; afterward, she headed to town to start her day, making people smile at the creations she'd made for Dora's Seashell Shop on The Bay.

* * *

Kat McConnell smiled, her heart happy as her sisters walked into her restaurant at dinner time. It was a busy time of day for Café By The Seaside, but today was a very important day for the McConnell sisters so her staff was taking care of things as she had dinner with Dora and Pearl.

After hugs she led them outside to the deck overlooking the ocean. She had reserved their favorite spot, the table at the lowest level of the stairway that zigzagged down the incline along the river. People came from all over to sit at this particular table.

Along the way, down the stairs they passed landings built for a single table, each with a view of the river making its way to the freedom of the sea.

"This is such a special spot," Dora said, smiling as she looked out toward the ocean, her golden blonde hair sparkled as it caught the gold of the setting sun.

"Yes it is," Pearl agreed, placing her arm around Dora's shoulders and giving her a hug. Pearl's soft pearl-toned hair and Dora's gold blonde hair mingled together as they took in the view.

Seeing her sisters so close made Kat smile, she understood what they were feeling, she felt it too. She stepped up beside them and placed her arm across theirs and leaned her vibrant rust-toned hair to theirs. "Everyone loves it and we know, other than her back porch, this was our sweet Olivia's favorite place to be." On Olivia's last lunch with all of them, Matt had carried her down the stairs to the table, settled her into her chair and then took that long walk back up to give them time together.

Yes, their dear friend had loved this spot and today was their third year without her. And their third year to keep this promise, getting together and remembering her with happiness, not sadness as she'd requested. Celebrating life and catching up on each other's busy lives, keeping their sisterly connection strong.

"Our Olivia was one smart lady," Kat said, smiling at Dora and Pearl. "Now, let's relax and enjoy this time together. Olivia knew we needed to do this since our lives keep us really busy."

Dora took her seat on the left side, her back to the wall as Pearl strode to the far side not minding her closeness to the edge of the landing. It was safe with the railings but she and Pearl knew Dora had her fears. Kat sat at the end of the table with her back to the ocean and her gaze on her sisters and the restaurant, she saw this view among others at her other restaurants often, and today it was her sisters she was here to see.

"This is wonderful as always," Dora said. "Who did

you have to kick out of this spot, a billionaire cowboy and his date?"

They all chuckled at that since they were surrounded in this area by huge ranches, wealthy cowboys—and cowgirls. The three of them were included in that group as their dad's ranch was huge here in Texas, and he had small acreage on Kawaii and also the Big Island of Hawaii.

Pearl smiled her amazing smile. "She's had this table reserved for us for months. But I'm glad because we have all been on the road hard this year—well me and Kat have been. You, our no traveling home-body sister, don't know what you're missing."

It was true. Pearl was a majorly successful photographer and an article writer who traveled all over the world. She was happily single, like Kat, and able to do what she wanted because of her amazing talent. Kat traveled also, but more in the USA, although her restaurants in Kauai and Kona on the Island of Hawaii were her most frequent places to travel. Like this one, they had stunning views. And Kona had the bay for deep sea fishing, which she absolutely loved, making Kona her favorite place to be. She'd even thought of making it her home spot but her family was here and that made this great island of Star Gazer her special place.

Their brother had taught them that working and

finding what you wanted out of life was an awesome thing. Their dad had basically not demanded that they go to college, though he had encouraged it. Their brother, yes, he was like their dad, an incredible rancher and a college graduate in agriculture and business that helped him be one of the best ranchers and producers around. Also, helped him manage their oil gurgling producing ranch better. Yes, their land was loaded with horses, cattle and oil.

Thankfully Matt had moved back to take the lead on the ranch, giving his sisters the space to do what they loved. And enabling their parents to travel when they felt like it. They were doing a lot of that now as they wished for and waited on grandbabies. Kat was thinking that would be happening soon with Matt and Kelley, but she and her sisters were not yet in the marrying mood.

Pearl, or Pearly as Matt used to call her because of her pearl-toned hair, was now a sought-after photographer and writer. She'd gone two years in college, then her love of photos had gotten her an amazing opportunity in the Florida Keys. Amazing photographs she'd taken while the family was there on a fishing trip, which Kat loved, had gotten her recognition when, on a spur of the moment action, she'd submitted them to a well-known fishing magazine. Instantly her work became a hit. It wasn't only the family fishing photos she'd taken but also the scenery and the snorkeling from below water that she'd submitted to another magazine. Those too had been a huge hit and her career using a camera to capture life. College had ended for her then as she almost instantly became a sought after photographer.

Add to that her talent of writing an article to match the photos, and Pearl McConnell was unstoppable. Beyond magazines, her photographs sold as pricey paintings to decorate the homes of the affluent and hotels countrywide. For a very amazing cost she even traveled to places to meet and take photos of the wealthy. She was independent and seeing the world on her terms, and came home in between. Like Kat, Star Gazer Island and their ranch here was still Pearl's home, although they weren't here all the time.

Kat loved cooking with as much love as Pearl had for photography. And had skipped college to take culinary classes all around the country from some of the best. She'd found her heart inside the kitchen. She had a natural skill in business also, and that had helped her take her skills to the next level. For that, she was thankful to have found her place in life. And now, with Olivia in mind, she smiled at her sisters. Olivia had wished her well in her love for making people smile with her food. And she'd accomplished that not merely through opening her restaurants but also by selecting great places with ideal atmospheres that attracted people.

It gave Kat and her sisters a place to celebrate life and this was their spot, and Kat was happy she had it. Olivia had been with them as they'd each found their place in life. She'd urged them on, cheered them on, and eaten here on this deck with them their first time. As if reading where her thoughts had gone, her sisters smiled gently.

Kat smiled and picked up the glass of sparkling champagne already waiting beside their plates and lifted it in the air between them, as her sisters did the same. "Today we celebrate our sweet friend Olivia's life and our blessing in knowing her and the joy and legacy of love she left us with."

They touched glasses, each took a sip, and looked out at the ocean, each with their own memories. In a few minutes they looked at each other with tears glistening in their eyes, then smiled as Olivia had hoped. Remember her not with grief but joy.

Pearl lifted her glass again, smiling. "One more toast to the love we feel right now. Onward and upward, let's get joyful, sisters."

That made them smile, touch their glasses again, and take a sip, this time feeling the happiness Olivia wanted them to feel.

Kat knew sweet Dora struggled with that sometimes but now she smiled, having fought off tears, and Kat was thankful she'd fought them off. Dora worried them sometimes, with the quiet life she lived, the seclusion they felt was too much. But getting her out and about was hard to do.

Kat set her glass down as did her sisters and she met Pearl's gaze and it told her she'd been watching Dora too. She laid her hands palm-up on the table toward each of her sisters and they both did the same as they all joined hands. Dora smiled, hopefully feeling the strength of all of them.

"Ladies, girlfriends, sisters, this is the start of a great evening. So, with smiles and remembrance of Olivia, let's have a fantastic evening meal and chat. No more tearing up. It's smile time. We're doing exactly what we promised we would do, not mourning but celebrating and making our dreams come true. And I have to say that I'm so thrilled we're doing this, celebrating life in Olivia's favorite spot—"

"Her favorite spot with us," Dora broke in. "Before our brother married her and it became being with him snuggled up on their back porch watching the stars and the moon beaming above."

"So true." Oh, how Olivia had loved moonbeams,

them, family, and most of all, their brother.

What would love like that feel like? Kat smacked that thought out of her mind, she wasn't looking. She had a great life and if there was a man out there for her he'd have to slam into her and reel her in with skill because she'd be fighting like a massive Blue Marlin fighting not to be reeled in. Most would say like a bull, but she knew both, and a Blue Marlin could fight with substantial strength and skill. And she was skilled.

"You are so right," Pearl agreed and Kat nodded, yanking her thoughts off of being a giant fish. "This was a great idea and I'm so glad you made this spot so we can celebrate our friend here, Kat. But now, we have to move forward in our conversation. When are you flying off to Hawaii?"

Thank goodness, a topic she was ready for. "Soon. I've been around and checked on all my restaurants in Texas so now it's time to visit my Hawaiin restaurants. You both know I'm a Kona lover. Spending time there fishing and testing recipes is like a vacation and inspiring time for me. Time there seems to slow down and I love it so I'm heading out in about a week."

"You do love it there," Dora said. "You brighten up when talking about both your Hawaiin restaurants but especially Kona. They're newer restaurants and probably need you there, but I think by your reaction that you need to be there too."

She smiled at her sister who hit it on target. "Yes, I do. I want them to be at the top of travelers' wish list when they make that flight to paradise. And I love it there, everything about it. Even the lava rock spread all across the island."

"And the fishing," Pearl added. "You love restaurants. But you love fishing in the ocean more than any woman.

"Yes," Dora said. "I've never seen anything but happiness sparking from you when thinking about Kona. You've both created wonderful lives. I'd go to Kona too if I was you."

Kat was shocked. "Come with me. I'm going there for three weeks minimum, perhaps four, and it could be longer this trip. I have amazing chefs at all my places, and managers too. So, I'm comfortable going, it's time to experiment with recipes. Dora, it's the beginning of April. Your vacationing customers aren't here yet, business will pick up in May, so let your helper take over and come out for at least a week—I'd say more but know you wouldn't do that. Even if you fly out for at least five days, allowing the other two days for travel. Come to Kona with me. Come fishing with me. Fishing for my favorite, Blue Marlin, is now in season. The way the island is shaped leaves the wonderful bay protected by the volcanos, making it an awesome place to fish. Or simply a place to enjoy on the beautiful, wonderful, calm bay that is deep almost instantly." Her excitement for Dora to go and her love of Kona radiated through her with excitement. "It's not as beautiful as Kauai but it would take time to show you all of Kauai's beauty. But, oddly I love the lava-ridden Island of Hawaii. The Big Island."

Dora looked from her to Pearl, there was a shocking spark of interest in her blue eyes.

Pearl laid a gentle hand on her arm. "Come on, do this, Dora. You need to step out a little. Kat will be there, and I would to, but I can't, work calls."

Kat wanted this. "Dad has designated his private jet for me on this trip so his pilots can also bring you home. No busy airports for you. You'll love it."

Dora smiled slowly and nodded. "I'll go with you."

Shock filled Kat. "Awesome," she exclaimed as she jumped up, Pearl beat her to her feet and they both wrapped their arms around their little sister.

This was going to be great. She and Pearl leaned back and looked into the startled eyes of Dora. She laughed at their looks. "Okay, I'm an oddball who finds joy in walking on my beach picking up shells and rocks. But I'm going to shake things up."

There it was done. They sat back down, knowing

they'd drawn attention from everyone. Kat grinned. "We're going to have a great time. And Dora, I feel Olivia smiling down at us right now. This is a special place. Our special place."

Dora's eyes grew bright and then they all looked back out to the sparkling moonbeam crossing the ocean and down the river as if coming right to them. It felt like a smile from heaven.

Oh what a wonderful night, Kat felt hopeful that maybe this was a first step out for Dora. A needed step.

CHAPTER TWO

Hawk Harrison walked across the beach of his newly purchased property to the large rock that bordered his land from his neighbor. The rock stuck out into the water like an almost perfect hard line between the properties. The land wasn't exceptionally large by Texas standards, totaling three hundred acres, with an older house that had huge potential. But, it this great private beach that added to the worth substantially and it's location was his instant selling point.

He could put a few cattle on it if wanted, but the lands location was the most appealing factor. He liked remodeling real estate. Transforming something old, giving it a fresh new look was a great start, but it was always the location that made the difference in big buys.

His brain always switched into the creation mode when he spotted a winning place. It went into overtime figuring out exactly how to make a statement that he'd been there. Yes, it sounded crazy to him but there was no denying that his worth came from his crazy never-stop-creating brain.

The best part was he enjoyed property development and house renovation. Making the right choices, creating a big draw to the people who came looking. He enjoyed seeing their reactions before they made a bid.

He especially loved that what he did didn't hold him down to any one area. Thus, he bought properties all over the country and sometimes, like this one, he lived in it while he oversaw the full transition himself. It was a pause for him only, a moment to feel the settling in of a place before he sold and moved to the next spot. He always moved forward.

Flying his helicopter over the land and seeing it from above gave him more perspective. He spottrd things that helped him understand it was a good buy or a no, noticing things he might have overlooked while walking such a large property.

Flying ranked among his favorite pastimes, particularly his early morning flights from this spot. He could fly to the airport, board his waiting jet and work while his pilots flew him to wherever his work happened to be that day. He'd owned this property for two weeks and had been working away until a few days ago. Now, he'd flown over this area two times getting to the airport in the early morning hours and both times he'd seen his neighbor. She walked in the early morning sunlight on the beach and once when he'd flown over after dark he believed he'd spotted her sitting on this rock in the moonlight.

He'd decided the time to meet his neighbor was today, actually she was one of the selling points influencing his buying decision. His acreage, only three hundred acres that by Texas standards was small and considered a large homeplace, not a ranch. Other states possibly, but Texas, especially out here near Corpus Christi area where ranches were huge and historical, small was the word for his acerage.

The historical King Ranch and others made even ten thousand acres look tiny. Some of the owners like the McIntyre's, the Valentine's, and the McConnell's, had ranches that also owned beach land here and were now, basically his neighbors, also a selling point.

The McConnell's were his actual next-door neighbors, putting a higher price tag on his property. He wa a bit confused as to why they hadn't bought it themselves but now he owned it and was glad. A high-level fixer-upper he recognized that, once finished, this

19

property's value would be significantly higher than the purchase price. And part of that would come from location.

Location, location, location always upped the price even more after his upgrades were made. He'd gotten lucky on the buy and the beauty of the beach and the town nearby made this his place to settle in for a while. He was glad to be here. This area drew him. Star Gazer Island was a pretty town on the bay. It had become very well known for the amazing Star Gazer Inn and its restaurant, and another restaurant, Cafe By The Seaside, that sat near the coast on the river that flowed into the ocean.

And his neighbor he hoped he was about to meet was the sister of the owner of the Cafe By The Seaside. He'd learned in his extensive research that Kat McConnell owned several cafe's including two in the Hawaiian islands, some of his favorite places to buy and remodel property.

However, it was his neighbor, Dora McConnell's early morning beach infatuation that intrigued him. Clearly an early riser, the sun had barely peaked over the horizon each time he'd spotted her. And why did she pull a small rolling ice bucket along with her each morning?

On his second time of spotting her, she'd been

sitting on the chest, bent over picking something up out of the sand as waves washed in over her feet. She'd looked up from where she sat and he'd given her a hand salute but she didn't wave back. Probably hadn't had time to lift her hand from the sand before he was past her.

She was one of three daughter's of the huge ranch owner and unlike her sisters who both had big businesses, because he'd researched the sought-after photographer Pearl McConnell also, who was all over the place on jobs. But Dora owned a quaint but well-known souvenir store in Star Gazer and lived in this small beach house on the far edge of the property. It was in its own little nook with its little beach area, basically secluded from everything. And it joined his property, separated by a large fence and this huge rock dipping out into the water.

The value of his land was upped because of the McDonnell's land and that had been the selling point of his buy.

Now, he'd decided it was time to introduce himself to Dora, let her know she had a neighbor she could trust. Let her know she would see him flying in and out often and not to worry. Introducing himself was the right thing to do. Meet the lady who obviously loved the morning and digging in the sand.

Also he was introducing himself so that she would realize who kept flying over and to ask if the helicopter was disturbing her mornings. If that were the case he could redirect his path and not cut across this corner of her land. Though it was apparent to him from all of his traveling and buying and selling in different parts of America that people took helicopter tours all the time. It was a pretty normal thing for owners along beach areas to have to put up with.

The moment he rounded, instead of climbing, the large rock he spotted her. She was standing there now, in the morning sunlight wearing a teal-toned tank top that showed off her toned, tanned arms and mid-thigh denim shorts that showed her small, short legs that seemed even shorter since her ankles were buried in the sandy water as the waves rolled in, surrounding her. Her hands were on her hips, her ice chest was a few feet behind her on the now wet shore leaving her alone there in the water, staring up at the rising sun.

It was a beautiful moment. Mentally he slapped his brain, he hadn't come here to be infatuated by his neighbor. He wasn't looking for an interest in a woman like that. He liked his life, his non-obligated, non-tied-down life. Yes, he was thirty-five years old and hadn't always been non-tied down. But for the last twelve years, he had been and he had no plans to make a change.

He pushed the thoughts away and was about to say hello when Dora spun, obviously having sensed she wasn't alone. Startling large blue eyes connected to him, and her long golden hair snagged him instantly as the breeze lifted strands to flow lightly all around her. He was stunned, in the sun on the beach, by the beauty before him in the middle of this early morning. Words were evaporated in that moment.

"Who are you? Stay where you're at," she said, it was a firm demand as she took a step back.

"I'm your new neighbor," he said, startled and not happy with himself. I didn't mean to alarm you." He gave an instant half grin hoping to ease the strain between him and the small woman. Her shoulders back, her gaze scanned him up and down in a quick flick. She looked very decisive, not terrified, thank goodness. "I'm Hawk," he added quickly. "And I fly the helicopter that you've seen in the early mornings. I was going to work this morning and decided it was time to come introduce myself. I wanted to make sure me flying over during your early morning walks isn't messing you up. If it is I can start flying a different route to the airport to catch my plane." He'd gotten it all out and she stood still, watching him.

He sounded a little off-kilter and for him that was highly unusual. But it was because those eyes of hers were holding his and as tiny as she was, she had not moved at all since her first step back. He wanted to tell her that there were some people she might need to turn and run from, at least be on the defensive.

Then it hit him, she was on defense as her unwavering blue gaze held his like glue. And that was fascinating. But it was the calm precision of her stare that had him totally startled and even more fascinated.

* * *

Dora hadn't realized she had a new neighbor. Yes, she'd known that the small, three hundred acres next door to their nearly one hundred thousand acres was for sale. She'd even considered buying it for herself instead of living on the corner of her parents' ranch, taking over this sweet ocean view and getting her own on the other side of the rock. But, she liked her little spot in the cove and her dad wanted her to stay. This cove was amazing with what washed up here in her small sandy blue water spot. Her own treasure trove of sea shells and other things that rolled in on the waves sometimes so she'd stayed.

Her artistic, creative mind loved walking early in the morning alone. And now she had a neighbor. She'd noticed the helicopter going over a couple of times. She initially believed it to be a tourist chopper; however, they rarely flew that early. Now she understood.

Her neighbor was stunning. He was tall, of course she was barely five foot four so everyone was tall to her. But he was at least as tall as her brother, so around six foot. He had straight dark brown hair that had a little wave at the top and as he stared at her the breeze ruffled his slightly wavy hair. The man had a strong jaw and lightning bolt eyes that had struck her hard with their electric golden tone. Her insides rattled as she held those eyes with hers. Her brain was crazy. She felt off balance and she realized suddenly that she hadn't said anything other than her warning of, "Who are you? Stay where you're at."

Now she forced her voice to remain steady and strong. "It's nice to meet you. I'm Dora McConnell, though you probably know my name since you were buying right next door." He looked like a man who knew where he stood in anything and everything, especially where he'd bought a piece of land.

"Yes, I know this is the McConnell property and since I buy real estate that was a draw for me. I knew that one day, when I decided to sell the property, this ranch will still be here and help keep the price up and stable. I'm pretty positive knowing that will help sell, am I right?"

He hitched a brow and she couldn't help but chuckle. "Yes, my father and family will never sell. Of that you can be certain. If you've done research and you must have since you paid a good sum for the land you bought. And some of that is because of where it's located, and as you thought this will never be sold."

"Yes, I did research. I buy property and look for property that has a sustainable, escalating price. I'll be updating before I sell. But I'll make sure you have great neighbors when I do. For now, it's me. But when I do sell it will be to someone trustworthy. Since you live here, around the rock at the edge of your father's large property. Which makes me wonder why y'all didn't buy the property."

"Honestly, my dad would have bought it but, well, the owner was his father's friend and he wouldn't sell to Dad. He said someone new needed to buy so there'd be new blood." She didn't say everything that her granddad's buddy had said. He'd hoped someone would move in next door and maybe one of those sweet little gals he loved like his own would fall in love. No way was she going to say that. Especially since she was the one who had taken over the little beach house. She had no plans for any such thing happening, and looking at the man standing before her, she looked like he felt the same way.

"New blood," he said as a slow grin crossed his expression.

Her insides roared like a mighty wave was coming in. What a grin the man had and that twinkle in his eyes.

"So he thought y'all were bad blood or he thought y'all needed neighbors for… what? Mates? Was your grandpa a matchmaker?"

She laughed, she couldn't help it. "Honestly, I have no idea. I was a little young when he made that statement. He died before I was of dating age but I have a feeling that what you say is right. Now the property has sold to you so no worries. Whatever my grandfather's friend was thinking, this is my own little spot right here."

He grinned. "It's a great spot and you're safe, I'm not looking to be matched up either and won't come wandering around or over the rock too much."

"Great." She looked from him to the sand around them. "Me and my seashells, seagulls, and the pelicans that fly in to visit do great here in our quiet place. I do have to say though that I wandered around the rock myself not too long ago. I wanted to see if there were any updates on the land and saw there were none. Do you have plans for it? I mean, the house. It's great, older. Like I said, it was my grandfather's friend and his family kept it all these years instead of selling it. They didn't come up much and obviously didn't do any updates."

"Yes, that's what I do and what you're saying is exactly what I thought. The setting is beautiful, the view is amazing."

Their eyes locked for a moment before he looked out at the ocean. She was glad because for an instant there she thought he was talking about her when he said the view. Of course she didn't want him thinking that because she wasn't looking. But, for that moment she had that feeling and turned her gaze also out to the ocean waves racing in. "You're going to get your feet wet if you don't step back," she warned.

"I'm barefooted too. Not often. I'm usually in my boots and jeans but today I'm on the beach and enjoying it."

"That's great. I would think if you enjoy buying property you need to have a feel for what to do with something before you redo it. For buyers' sake."

He looked at her, that smile returning. "Exactly. I have a pretty good vision and done a lot... of houses."

She caught his hesitation. She had a feeling, because she knew the land he'd just bought wasn't cheap, that he must be very good at what he did. She liked that he wasn't trying to use it as a benefit right now.

"I imagine since you pick up a seashell and make a treasure out of it that you have vision too." It wasn't a question but a statement. She smiled at him, couldn't help it. "I do. In my family, we're like a family of visions. Me, I like taking a sea shell and making something uniquely special. My sister Pearl likes taking a picture and makes a beautiful statement. My sister Kat, whose restaurants are known for their amazing views and atmosphere, has a knack for creating captivating spaces. Then she adds in her food, yes, she has a vision, an amazing vision. Both of them do. As does my brother Matt, for the ranch."

He'd turned toward her with his hands on his hips, his lean hips. His feet were like hers, covered in swirling water. They were only about two feet apart and for an instant the draw she felt toward this man was undeniable. But she denied it.

She swallowed, the dry mouth had suddenly swamped her. He, as if caught in the moment too, stared at her. Her alert system went up, she took a step back in the water, tripped in the muddy sand and down she went.

Or was falling when her new neighbor grabbed her arm, then swept her into his arms as he too stumbled in the water, probably from hurrying to catch her. Now on a roll they plummeted together into the low tide and sand as a wave washed over them.

Water in mouth she laughed hard as the comedy of the rescue raced over her. She sat up, water dripping off of her and sopping wet hair drenched over her shoulders, she looked at her neighbor. Her *amazingly* handsome neighbor sitting in the waves, arms resting on his knees, grinning at her.

"Well, that was a way to get to know each other." Hawk laughed too then stood up, reached down and took her arm as she started to stand.

"I can do it," she said, noticing the feel of his hand more than she wanted to.

"I need to make sure to get you up out of the water since I'm the one who didn't save you from landing in it."

From his touch all the way to her toes she was tingling as her gaze met his. A sharp feeling of what... wanting more? *Speak,* her inside voice demanded.

"Yes, that was a mess up on my part so I'm sorry I took you down too."

This man, this amazing, attractive, draw-her-like-honey-to-a-bee man, caused her insides and brain to go berserk. "Maybe we should walk to the shore," she said, and he grinned. Then holding her arm they walked to the firmer sand. The sand with no muddy sinkhole like she'd just fallen into and didn't need to fall in again.

CHAPTER THREE

Hawk had lost it. Not just his balance but his sanity. He wasn't here looking for romance, certainly not with his new neighbor. The last thing he needed to do was cause a problem in her life or his. There was no denying he was attracted to her despite trying not to be. So that meant getting back to business. "It's been nice meeting you, Dora. Sorry we had to roll in the water together but I'm glad I was here, well I take that back. If I hadn't been here you probably wouldn't have stumbled in the water. Sorry about that."

She laughed again, she had an amazing laugh. It was gentle but resounding and unstoppable it seemed until she found a breath. That breath noticeably calmed her. Her smile remained. "It was nice meeting you too.

Hopefully, our next meeting won't be so salty."

He laughed this time. "Only if we want it to be. I do have swim trunks on. You, however, now have that soaked tank top and shorts. But—" He paused, his gaze scanning her small drenched body. "I'm going to shut up and head on out. If you need anything I'll be over there working today. But you'll know when I'm not because you're an early bird like me and will see me flying out." They were alike on being early risers. He liked seeing the sun come up and watching it go down too, and working in between. Everyday was a great day when he was busy.

He turned and headed back around the rock. He didn't look back and was glad he didn't. No, he didn't need to leave any more signs of attraction.

The woman was his new neighbor, Dora, as in Melvina Eldora Smith, her great, great, great, maybe another great grandmother who had been a mail-order bride to get away from terrible blame for her parents and uncles deaths as a baby. Sometimes the history he read before buying was ridiculous. Her many greats grandmother's history was really stupid. But Eldora survived and lived a long and happy life once she got away from the accusations of her aunt and all those who didn't stand up to the allegations that she'd killed three people before the age of one. If Eldora was as direct as her ancestor Dora, he knew why she'd survived. She was small but tough. And, probably had a way about her like Dora. A good way, and as much as he wanted to deny it he liked it.

* * *

Dora arrived at her brother Matt and his brilliant wife Kelley's amazing home. Her sister-in-law pulled open the large door and greeted her with a hug before she had time to ring the doorbell.

"Come on in, we're so glad you're here. I hear from your sisters that you are going to go to Hawaii for a visit. That's wonderful. Everyone is so excited. You're going to have a blast and see a new place."

Goodness, so everyone knew already and were probably shocked that she was flying that far. "Yes, I decided I would, even though as you probably already heard I'm not the big traveler in the family like everyone else is."

Kelley patted her arm and chuckled. "I get it. But you know me, now that I can actually walk into buildings again and have contracts to build homes and buildings, I have to fly and love that I'm back to normal. Thanks to your sweet brother who helped me when I needed it. I adore the call of adventure and you're about to have your own."

Her beautiful sister-in-law had a horrible experience of a home caving in on her but her father had saved her. She'd met Matt when she'd bought the property of their ancestor, Katie Pearl. Her family somewhere down the line had sold the property. Kelley had researched it and bought it because of its history. The land they still owned and where Matt had gone to live was the property of her namesake, Melvina Eldora and Mathew McConnell, her mail-order husband. Matt was there still mourning his loss of Olivia almost three years after losing her and he and Kelley met. She needed Matt's help and they fell in love even though Matt wasn't looking or thinking about ever falling in love again. But Kelley had been living outside the same way their grandmother had lived after a tornado killed her dad and trapped her with a fear of going inside. Matt had worked to help Kelley reenter four walls just like their cowboy great, great, great grandfather Treb helped Katie reenter the house he helped her rebuild.

The thought always filled Dora with pride for the ancestors she came from who had overcome hardships and struggles to find fulfilling love. And that was what Matt and Kelley had found together.

Will I ever know love like that? The question raged through her suddenly, and she wanted it, despite telling herself she didn't. Katie and Kelley both found the courage to walk back inside a closed in room. Dora had never known anything so hard and yet, she never put herself out there to take a chance.

Dora took no chances, couldn't imagine that feeling. Like them she knew people who were claustrophobic. Kelley and Katie had been so bad they'd lived outside with only a top cover open on all sides, not even a tent. But they'd both finally stepped up and faced their fear. Could she ever face her fear that no one other than herself knew about? Could she step out from her comfort zone?

Kelley was now back to doing what she was a master at, designing and building homes and businesses with large glass ceilings and windows, which is what helped her get back inside buildings and get back to her creating the amazing creations for others to enjoy. This house was one of those creations. As they walked down the long, wide hallway with a thin skylight, they entered the large living space and kitchen area where three huge sky windows, as Kelley called them, let the light shine in. And it was the perfect time of day where the sun had slipped slightly toward its downward trip to sunset. That angle sent the beautiful jeweled ornament that hung from the ceiling, a few feet away, into a sparkling array of glittering colors dancing across the room.

Breathtaking wasn't even a good enough word to describe the beauty. The ornament was made by a spectacular ornament maker in Mule Hollow, Texas, who created amazing affordable ornaments for everyone but also created ornaments made from real jewels that were bought by many and also auctioned off like this one had been at a huge price that all proceeds went to help a need. This one had helped a home for abused women and their children, No Place Like Home, there in that small town of Mule Hollow. But Matt had gone there determined to buy this for this room so that Kelley would always have a memory of her father's love for her. Her father had literally thrown her out of the way of a roof caving in and saved her while giving his life for her. This was a show of her love for him and her achievement of overcoming the fear that had held her back. And it was also a reminder of amazing Olivia who had wanted the man she loved to find new love after she was gone.

That death had been hard on Matt who had married Olivia knowing she was going to die from the cancer that she had but he'd done it anyway. He'd suffered but found himself again while helping Kelley. In all of that, Dora's strong brother had been able to return here to Star Gazer to take over the ranch, running it like he'd always planned on doing before sorrow and loss had taken him away. Away to meet his destiny which was Kelley.

Now, the sparkles spun around the room and she looked at the glow on her smiling family. Love was the message of the sparkles. The everlasting sparkle of love. Everyone was smiling at her now as she walked in. And she knew instantly that they were grinning because like Kelley they were happy she was going on a trip.

She laughed. "Yes, I'm going to Hawaii. Don't all of you look so shocked."

"And," her grinning dad said. "You're going to go deep sea fishing. On a boat, in very deep water."

She hesitated. "Yes, and are you wanting to make me not go by telling me all of that?" The room full of family busted out in laughter.

Her dad strode over and put an arm across her shoulders. "No, I'm not. You are a tough, tiny cookie, so you go and have fun. I'm thrilled you're stepping out. It's a good thing sometimes. There is a world out there, Dora. Not just in our little corner of the ranch, where you hide out and find all your jewels for your little store here on Star Gazer Island. Yes, you make many, many visitors happy with your amazing designs they can take home for memories, but it is high time for you to make some memories too. If you need ranch time while you're there go out to the ranch and check out the updates we've made." He gave her a squeeze and a smile. "Your sister stays clear of the ranch while at either island."

"She's busy," Dora said, taking up for Kat, not that she needed it.

"Yes, she is." He grinned, walked back to put his arm around her mom's waist. "I was once too busy." He looked at her smiling mom, the woman who won his heart with that smile.

"He's right, dear, though nothing your dad said was supposed to be insulting. We are simply happy you're going on a trip. And Rand does a great job on the ranch and doesn't need an overseer." She elbowed their dad in the rib and he laughed. He hired the best and they knew it. Ross Willington couldn't be a better rancher, and he loved the freedom he had on the Islands, overseeing both ranches very well.

This was true, Dora's parents loved what she did and enjoyed having her around. But suddenly it struck her that they were right, she did hide out in her own world most of the time and Olivia had seen it too and asked her to step out and explore life... It was true she had a life in a very small area. She sucked in a breath, put her hands on her hips. "Yeah, it is time that I start doing things. So, I'm taking this step and glad to see y'all loving it so much."

Pearl came to her side and gave her a hug. "You're

going to love it more than you think. You'll find some treasures there to bring back to share with others and I know that's what you're all about. Finding beauty in small things and making people smile when they see what you've created."

Pearl got it all right in that statement. That was how Dora felt so she hugged her. "Thanks, that's what I love to do."

Kat came over and gave her a hug. "We're going to have fun. I promise."

Dora forced a smile, feeling suddenly the pressure of what she was about to do. Her family's shock was a wake-up call.

She needed to do this. It was definitely time. Way past time.

CHAPTER FOUR

Hawk arrived at the renowned Star Gazer Inn restaurant that he'd heard so much about. He walked out onto the back patio and was immediately greeted by a very beautiful, middle-aged woman he instantly assumed was Alice, the owner and Jackson's mother.

"Welcome to Star Gazer Inn," she said, with cheerfulness. "I'm Alice McIntyre Roark, the owner of the Inn and co-owner of this wonderful restaurant. You're new in town. Are you meeting someone for lunch?"

"I'm Harper Harrison, but I go by Hawk. I'm very glad to meet you, Alice. I'm actually here to have lunch with your sons. At least Jackson for certain. He said the others might be able to make it."

"It's so great to meet you. Jackson and Nina told me you bought two of Nina's paintings and moved to town after seeing the scene she'd painted from our property."

"That's right. Her painting was so amazing that I had to come see the territory myself. And found the house on the bay."

"I'm so glad you've come. He's waiting at a table near the railing so your view will be wonderful. He told me that you bought the property out there down past my son Riley and his wife Sofie's Glamping camp. You've bought a beautiful property and I love the family's father who lived there for so many years. He would be so happy that you have bought it. You are single, right?"

Her question startled him then he remembered Dora's story about why the owner hadn't sold it to the McIntyre's. He smiled, though he felt a bit awkward. "Yes, ma'am, I'm single and travel a lot so I won't be here as much as most people." There, maybe that would help stop what he thought she was thinking. "I love the property too. I'm going to do some remodeling and get it ready to sell. It will be noteworthy if my plan is like this place. You've done an amazing job. Jackson told me about the great remodeling update you and your husband did here."

She started walking and talking and he followed. "Thank you and from what Jackson told me about you that is a huge compliment. You do properties everywhere. So, I appreciate your compliments. You'll have to come inside and see the rest when you have time. My amazing husband, Seth, he loves remodeling and left the Fortune Five Hundred world to do it when he's not fishing on the bay. Anyway, I know you're here to talk to this handsome cowboy."

Jackson had already stood up and gave her a smile and a hug. "Thanks, Mom."

"Yes, thanks and it was great meeting you too," he added. She smiled, spun away then hurried back toward the new customers already there waiting to be seated. He looked at the grinning Jackson. "She's wonderful."

"Yes, she is. And she loved meeting you. So, have a seat." They shook hands then sat down.

He looked out over the gardens and pebble walks and the low stone wall between the inn and the beach and sparkling water. "This is an amazing view." He could see far across the bay to the outline of Corpus Christi. He flew over all of this in his helicopter but close up it was better than from above. He'd made a great buy and he knew it. The town itself was a huge draw.

"I'm glad you moved in. I told you it would be a

smart buy."

"And you, Mr. Incredible Cattleman, were right. You know cattle and land, just like my research said you did." One thing about Hawk was his hawk's eye for property. His nickname he'd gotten early on was because he could zero in on things. His in-depth research helped him find perfect areas that, done right, brought in top-dollar buys. Jackson had a good eye too.

Jackson grinned. "That's what I've been told but I learned it from my dad, the best there is. So it makes me proud to represent him since we lost him a few years ago."

He nodded. Having heard how the rancher and talented cowboy had been taken down in the Frio River trying to save a cow. His sons' hadn't been able to save him and had to overcome the loss. He understood that to some degree. Not that his dad had been amazing, no, he'd been degrading and walked out on him and his mom when Hawk was an adolescent. That was when Hawk had known he had to do things for himself. And Hawk had fought hard to be where he was at now and hadn't slowed down, though there was a time that he should have. That time was done, and here he was, moving forward as usual, conquering a new area.

"One of my brothers is tied up at the moment. Riley is having a big event at his camp out near your place and couldn't take a moment away from the glamping ladies that were coming but he wants to meet you, just can't today."

Another cowboy walked up at that moment and held his hand out. "Hello, I'm Dallas, and glad to get here to welcome you to town."

This cowboy was strong and tough looking. "Glad to meet you too. You're the bull rider."

Dallas nodded as he sat down. "I am, or was. I'm glad I gave it up when I did, I can still move around easy, not crippled up. When you have kids, you know how important that is. Though, even if I was a beat-up old bull rider, I'd still have fun with my boys, riding and roping and wrestling, I might hurt more while doing it." He grinned.

Hawk liked the man, felt a jolt inside knoeing he would never know the joy of having kids of his own. He pushed that thought away and focused on the now, "I've already hung Nina's painting on the wall. It's a stunning piece of art."

Jackson smiled like a proud husband. "Her love for her painting and creating drives her. It's still wild that her painting brought you to our area. And the spot you bought proves you have good taste."

"Thanks, I love what I do too." He was driven by his love of traveling and finding new remodels. Sadly, that drive came after his early marriage fell apart.

"We'll have you out to the ranch soon so you can meet everyone and see our place," Jackson said. "It's a thirty minute or so drive. And you'll be invited to come to the major cattle and horse sale we'll have in a couple of months. You'll want to come out and meet cattlemen and others from all over Texas. Might find another piece of property."

Dallas grinned. "My brother thinks you're obsessed."

"He's right," Hawk said and they all laughed. "I'm a buyer and driven to take a place and make it spectacular." It was true he wa proud that his vision for things came true… "But I do that with hard work and great people who work with me to create my vision. I don't take any of it for granted." He made a great living at it, but, whether he did or not, he enjoyed taking a property and making it shine. Taking something used, maybe abused or forgotten and bringing it back to life. He had a huge group working for him enabling him not to have to be everywhere at one time.

His foremen could achieve his goals at each place enabling him to fly from one place to the other. He had a big trip this coming weekend and was looking forward to it as always. But right now, he needed to get to know his new neighbors. People he thought he could actually be friends with... really good friends. Odd to say but for him it was something he hadn't been compelled to seek out in a very long time.

He moved around so much and most things he did were in and out, redo and sell and on to the next project. The next state, country. He loved to move around. So, why was he thinking Star Gazer Island was different?

It suddenly struck him, having a home base could be beneficial for him. At least check out the idea and make moving on this time take a little longer than usual. Give himself time to see if he could stay somewhere longer than a project. For some reason this place called to him. His mind instantly turned to his neighbor. The woman seemed so comfortable out there alone in the sand and waves.

She'd seemed at peace and he liked it. Peace was something he hadn't felt in a very long time. It suddenly tugged at him hard.

"You should go down and see the Glamping camp down the beach from you," Jackson said, bringing Hawk's thoughts back to the here and now. "It's pretty cool what they have going on."

"I was thinking about it. I've seen it when I fly over and yesterday noticed along the road there were a lot of campers waiting to get in."

"It's the Glamping ladies," Dallas said, grriningl.

"They're the ones that brought Sofie into Riley's life because she used to run the group. They helped Riley know Glamping was definitely the way to go with his camp."

Jackson smiled. "And that Sofie was the woman for him."

The two brothers looked completely happy for their brother on finding love and his business venture. "Interesting. I might have to drive over there, or walk down the beach might be the better way. If they don't mind." Why was he wanting to go look at it? He wasn't going to buy a property to put a Glamping camp on. That was an amazing thing but not of interest to him. But, he was curious, as always on anything that had to do with land. And a walk down the beach would mean having to go around that rock and maybe seeing his neighbor once more. That thought struck him hard. He wouldn't mind seeing his neighbor again. Why? Whether he wanted it to be or not, the thought had been with him ever since he met her.

* * *

Dora was out early in the morning, after having spent the evening before at her brother's and enjoying herself immensely.

Now she stood with her feet in the water and her arms wrapped around her waist, gazing out at the beautiful sun rising. The soft, gentle waves, the pale blue sky rising into the gentle orange line appearing in the distance, hovering, hanging on the peace of the morning. She could tell by the morning light that the sunset would be amazing. And tonight, she would be out to watch the sunset. Sitting on the rock, her neighbor's and her rock. It crossed both lines and she'd had it to herself for years to watch the awesome sunsets or to enjoy on a moonlit night.

She heard the helicopter, glanced to the left as it rose up into the sky. In a quick foward push it flew out over the water in front of her then dipped her way for an instant. She spotted Hawk as he lifted his hand in a wave before he flew down the beach. It was quick and she didn't have time to even wave back.

Did she want to?

Yes, she did. The thought lingered as the waves rushed in and swirled around her ankles. She had hoped to see her new neighbor again. She'd only met the man once, so what was wrong with her? She watched the helicopter disappear down the coast and wondered how the people at the camp enjoyed seeing it. Then it was gone. Sighing, she gathered up her ice chest full of beautiful shells. She called her spot the catching spot for the most beautiful along the beach. It was as if amazing shells came to her little cove so they could get new life in her store. She saw amazing beauty in the shells and starfish. It was truly a blessing to stand here, pick one up and see what she could do to make someone want to buy it in a beautiful way. They were God's creations but she loved using the creative brain she'd been given to give her touch to them in inspired ways.

She let that thought take over instead of thinking about where the helicopter had gone. Or letting the temptation take over of going around the rock to see if there were any amazing shells over there. It had been a while since she'd done that. But suddenly there was more draw to trespass on the neighboring land than usual. She pulled back hard on the thought and stayed on her side where she belonged. It was time to head inside so she walked to her porch, slipped out of her sandals and rinsed her feet off at her outdoor water spray, then walked up the steps. Work in her store called and an hour later she pulled her SUV into the last parking slot at her business, leaving the spaces closest to her door for customers.

Feeling invigorated she got out and hurried to the door, had it unlocked quickly, then she strode inside. *This* was her creative spot she'd made for visitors to come in and find a treasured memory to take home with them. In these four walls she had found peace again. Peace that had once been disrupted, but no more. She got the cash out of her safe and placed it in the old-fashioned cash register. Yes, she took every kind of credit card, but this was a special piece of history that she loved having around. That done, she stood there, knowing it was going to be a slow day. There might only be one or two shoppers for revenue. She might have friends drop by to chat, it was the time of year she should use to explore more. Venture outside of her comfort zone but she hadn't. Until now.

Now she was going to do it. Step out and do a trip. She'd be leaving at the end of the week and thinking about it brought excitement to her.

Shock of all shocks. She looked around her store, home. Her place. Her safe spot, again, though it had once been threatened she'd taken it back. Hidden here inside, but now, she was about to step out of it. Just for a few days and she'd be with her sister and they'd have fun.

She was excited but suddenly her brain went to the helicopter and the handsome man who waved at her before zipping off into the rising sun, where had he been headed?

The door jingled and some customers came in taking her thoughts away from where they'd gone and where she didn't want them to go. She greeted the ladies, thrilled to have them here she walked over to help them find what they wanted or needed. This was who she was and why she did what she did. She'd never felt out of place or drawn anywhere else. She was at peace here.

But, again, Olivia's sweet voice rang in her head. "Dora, you never know what's out there until you go find out. Look at me, I wanted to but I can't. So, if you don't do it for yourself, do it for me." Those had been Olivia's words, but now she also heard words that hadn't really been spoken but she felt that Olivia would be urging her to go on an adventure. "That's what I made your sweet brother do and look at him now."

The words hung in the air surrounding Dora.

It was true. She could only imagine her sweet friend smiling because the man she loved had taken her to be his wife, even knowing he was going to lose her. Their love story was strong, but Olivia wanted him to move forward after she was gone. Matt had loved her so much. To distract her from the pain of her cancer that medications couldn't erase, he would carry Olivia out to the swing and they would cuddle together and talk about the places she wanted to see, the places she hoped he would see one day with someone else.

Those were the places Matt went to for almost two

years after losing Olivia and he took her with him in his heart and no one else.

Then unable to come home to Star Gazer he went to the old ranch to start over and there he'd met Kelley. In helping Kelley overcome her fear of enclosure he'd fallen in love, opened his heart again. That had enabled him to move forward just like Olivia so wanted him to do.

Love like that struck Dora in the heart. What would it feel like to love like that?

To *be* loved like that?

Her customer asked her a question, drawing Dora back to reality, thank goodness. Dora smiled broadly, feeling even more comfortable and at ease about her trip.

She was actually going to step out of her comfort zone just a little bit and spend five days somewhere that she thought she would enjoy. Yes, she had been told by her sister that the Island of Hawaii or as it was called the Big Island, wasn't anywhere near as beautiful as Kauai, but still, it had its beauty that drew Kat to love it most. The amazing town of Kona, where the wonderful pier with boats could take Kat out fishing in the deep bay that was protected from hard winds by the tall volcanoes. Then she could come back to her restaurant and cook fresh catch for anyone. She bought her fish from the locals but still enjoyed getting out and experiencing the water, the sun, and the atmosphere of trying to catch one of many of the fish there were to catch in March. April wasn't the best time to catch a Blue Marlin but they were there and that was always one of her sister's favorite catches.

Kat just loved being on the boat. It thrilled her and obviously gave her a wonderful feeling because going to Kona on the Big Island was her sister's favorite place to be. Even though she loved the beauty of Kauai and here on the coast of Texas, Kat had been drawn to Kona most. It was the lava-ridden volcanic island that had Kat's heart, and Dora was finally going to go and see it. Maybe soon she'd go check out Kauai.

She might fall in love with traveling and have to hire a store manager. She made enough money to hire more help than the two ladies who were stepping in while she was gone. But would she?

CHAPTER FIVE

After being gone for two days, Hawk arrived back home and decided to go for a walk on the beach. He put his thigh length shorts on, a T-shirt, and jogging shoes and headed out the door. Instantly, like a few days ago when he'd traded in his starched jeans, shirt, and boots for this outfit, he felt a relaxing calm sweep over him. Doing business could be stressful even when driven by the need. He strode out to the beach and breathed in the fresh air. He was glad he was doing this.

A plane flew over in the distance, and he was glad he wasn't up there at this moment. Yes, he had pilots who flew him all over the country while he worked. He had no one to bother him and it was how he'd worked for years. But his favorite time was in his helicopter, him flying it. But in this moment, as he stood there not thinking about what his new property was going to be when he finished it or what property he was going to buy. No, he was only thinking that the sun beginning to set before him on the topaz water was beautiful.

.Earlier he'd lifted up into the air in his helicopter and headed home. He'd been startled realizing he'd actually called this place home. He hadn't called any property home since he'd found his ex-wife and another man together in his house having an affair.

He thought about it now, staring out over the ocean. She'd thought he was a laid-back, good-time man who could give her anything she wanted when they met. He worked long hours to provide for them. Now, he worked because he was driven for the last twelve years to do what he did best, remodel and sell.

He took the blame for his failed marriage, but still, no matter what, she should have talked to him about her feelings, not gone behind his back like she'd done. She'd actually been relieved when he'd walked in and found the two of them together. Relieved because she was then free.

And so was he.

And awakened to the reality that he didn't want anything like that happening again. So, he'd thrown himself into his passion, his work, and now, he was at the top. Everyone knew his name in the world of rebuilding and perfection.

But standing here now, he decided to not think about all of that. He just wanted to walk on the shores of his new beach home and take it in. Not wanting to bother his neighbor he walked the opposite direction from the large rock. The rock that put him a mere few feet from probably seeing her out there gathering her treasures.

He pushed that thought away, seeing her hair glistening in the setting sun like it had on the morning in the rising sun. He bet she was smiling like he'd caught that morning. And the morning he'd dipped the chopper to say hello. She'd been a little shocked looking that day. And that was why he was walking away tonight.

She'd been on his mind a lot. There was no denying it. He had been married for only a year before it all fell apart. Now he had no worries about anyone other than himself. He did what he wanted to do and he had no personal obligations of any kind.

And that had been fine. But as the sun dipped a bit more he stopped walking, turned and headed back toward the rock. Why?

Because he was a free man and had been for a very long time. If he wanted to see if his neighbor was enjoying this beautiful evening, he would. He might take a moonlight walk to see the Glamping camp. If he saw Dora, he'd tell her he was going to do it tomorrow before the sunset and maybe she might want to go with him.

He made it to the rock and slipped off his running shoes and stepped into the water. Hearing movement he looked up and caught Dora as she'd just made it up onto the rock from her side. She was standing, looking down at him. His heart did a jump.

"So you like the sunset too?" she asked as she sank to sit, placing her hands behind her as she leaned back on them, holding his gaze.

"Yes," he said, grinning. "I wasn't expecting to find you up there. Thought you'd be on the beach like you are in the morning."

She chuckled, it rang gently out into the evening. "I can see what's in the water with me in the morning. When the sun sets, the water is a little deeper and well, I don't want my bare feet there in the dark. I'm a chicken when it comes to that."

Realizing that she had a point, he looked down in the calf-high water that was now growing darker by the second as the sun dipped. "I guess I'm the dummy."

She hitched a shoulder. "No, you're braver than me. *And* bigger and stronger, and if a stingray decided to slap you with its tail you could probably handle the sting better than me. *Though* if a shark mistook your leg for a fish, maybe it wouldn't drag you away."

He laughed. "You are purely optimistic."

"Well, you're the one in the water and I didn't want you to panic. But, if you'd like to join me up here there's plenty of room. The moonlight on the water after the sun goes down is a vision all its own."

She was a vision sitting there with the glimmer of the sun's last rays before dipping behind the horizon. "Sure." Without hesitation he took the invite and stepped from rock to rock getting up to the higher level of the large rock that had just enough flat area for two.

She scooted over slightly and he sat down, propping his wet legs before him on the rock and leaning back with his hands behind him, his palms flat against the rock like she sat. He looked at her and she smiled back.

"You didn't slip so that's good. You have great balance."

"Thankfully I do. I climb around on roofs and other places when checking out property or remodeling."

"Interesting."

Yes, she was. "So, do you often sit out on this rock at night all alone?" It suddenly worried him. Not that it was his business to worry but she was a small lady. And the rocks could be slippery and the waves could come in higher. He hadn't come out at night and wasn't sure how deep or far in the water came in a high tide.

She cocked her head to the side. "I do it often. When I want but I'm on my side of the rock so no worries. I'm not trespassing."

He smiled at the sarcastic ring in her voice. "That wasn't exactly why I was asking."

"I know but I think, well, I can do what I want when I want."

That was blunt. "Yes, you can, obviously." She might be small but she had a mind of her own. Even though she seemed quiet. As if to answer his unspoken question she looked back out over the water, then leaned her head back and stared up at the now rising moon. It was huge. The moonlight glistened over the water as if it was a gigantic bouncing ball that if they stood they could step from the rock, walk a short distance over the water and into it. "I get it. That is some kind of moonlight."

"Yes, it is. Beauty at its best and this week is special. It will rise up higher but right now it is astonishing."

He looked across his shoulder at her as she looked up at the moon. They sat close and she was smaller so he was looking down slightly at her. Then her gaze met his and moments stopped.

"I feel like I'm sitting beside a giant," she said, softly, teasingly.

"You are small." She was, but she had an expansive ambiance about her.

"I am. But, don't let that hold me back out here. I do what I want, when I want. Being small puts me closer to the sea shells I love hunting for."

Loving her quiet sense of humor he held her gaze, her indigo-blue eyes sparkling like jewels in the incredible moonlight. He didn't speak for a moment, just stared. He'd never met someone who drew him like this woman did.

He needed to back up, he hardly knew her and she was his new neighbor. She was just being friendly. So where had his crazy mind gone?

She looked away, back out to sea. "I am a loner. I also get that from my small grandmother from way back. Her name was Katie Pearl and she lived through a lot back then. A tornado came through and killed her dad leaving her with a fear of being enclosed. She lived outside for a while until a cowboy came along and helped her rebuild her cabin so she could build up courage to go inside again. It's a good story passed down through the ages to our family. She stayed outside because she couldn't go inside. Me, I love it outside."

"Great story and I got the feeling you loved it out here."

"I don't know if you've met my brother but he lost his sweet wife, mine and my sisters' best friend. It happened a little over three years ago and will soon be four years when the diagnosis came in that she wouldn't live. Matt realized he was going to lose her and he did. After taking a nearly two-year hiatus, carrying Olivia with him in his heart. They talked about those places while they cuddled up together on their back porch enjoying the moonlight, knowing she would never make the trips together. So, I think of her often in moments like this."

He was startled by her opening up to him but realized that he'd probably interrupted her thoughts when he'd walked out here. "I'm so sorry for all of your loss. She sounds like a lovely lady."

"She was. But I've learned that sometimes whether we know it or not there is a plan. Olivia couldn't live but she lived life with passion while here. And made us all make promises with her for after we lost her. Matt couldn't live up to his promise of finding love again or living here where they'd shared their love. So he went to the ranch in central Texas where our ancestors started."

It was obvious that sitting in this beautiful moonlight helped Dora open up. Hawk enjoyed hearing her story and knew some of it from his research, but listening to it told with heart and love for the friend and sister-in-law lost touched him. He was drawn to the lady sitting beside him. "He did what he needed to do." He'd done what he'd needed to do after his divorce but his love had been destroyed after being cheated on. This was different, this was true love.

"Yes, and we all understood. He didn't want to come back to Star Gazer Island, so there he went. Somewhere in history the land that Katie Pearl and her father lived was sold so we still owned our land beside it that came from my namesake Melvina Eldora Smith, so that was where he went to take over running that part of the ranch. She had a history too, a little sad and funny but anyway that's off the subject. Kelley had bought the property because she'd read about Katie Pearl and her fear of going inside after the tornado killed her dad and buried her beneath the house that she had to get free from. Kelley had also had a similar thing happen to her. She was a renowned homebuilder but could no longer go inside so she lived in an open area with only an awning over her living space and drove a Jeep with no top."

"She builds the glass houses. I see it when I fly over and in what I do I've read about her creations and even toured one."

Dora smiled, his pulse sped up at her joy. "That's

my new sister-in-law, but when she met my brother she couldn't step inside. Like Katie Pearl, her dad had saved her from a home falling on her and she lived like that until she found the property of my ancestor and her story drew Kelley to Katie's homeplace. We all think that Olivia was smiling down on Matt. Because he knew he had to help Kelley, like he hadn't been able to help Olivia. He is an amazing man, a great helper and he helped Kelley overcome her fear. She rebuilt the old home with glass ceilings and walls so that she could step inside and have no claustrophobia. Now she is known for her creations of being able to sit in the house and look up at the heavens like we are now but with glass. And we're all so happy that they married and my brother was able to go back to running the ranch and Kelley was able to take up her love of creating amazing homes."

"Yes, it is stunning." It was, the lady's creations were pure art.

"She is now in demand. Her homes are wanted. You just never know what God's plan is, He works in mysterious ways."

Hawk took that in. "Yes." He couldn't say more than that. "So, your other ancestor, the one you're named after. What is her story?" He knew the story from his research but wondered how she'd tell it.

Dora laughed in the moonlight and his insides

stumbled. He'd never felt that before.

"I'm Dora and I'm named after my ancestor whose name was Melvina Eldora Smith, as I said earlier. The story goes, from her Aunt Millicent, that from the ill-fated day of her birth, she killed three people before the age of one: her mother at birth, her father of a broken heart, and her poor, poor uncle Mutt outside a bar with a runaway buggy. This left Aunt Millicent blaming Eldora for killing her husband because he got drunk—it was more than likely that Aunt Millicent had the man drinking all the time. This left Eldora being raised by her angry aunt who took everything out on her. It's a sad story, but then, thank the good Lord, Eldora became a mail-order bride. She got on a stage coach and showed up in Wishing Springs, fell in love with my ancestor Mathew, and history was made. Eldora is who I'm named after, but like her, I'm not a killer."

He laughed, totally stunned by the story the first time he'd read it and now hearing it from her as she talked and looked at him with those sparkling, humorous eyes.

"I don't carry a pistol like Katie did but I live a quiet life here in my corner of the ranch. So just relax I won't shoot you, but I do know how to kick you in the right place if you make a move I don't like."

He grinned. This woman had a quiet but wild sense

of humor. "Do you get a lot of laughs when you tell these kind of stories at your store?"

She hitched up a shoulder. "Sometimes, but in all honesty, I don't often talk about my history. But I haven't ever sat here in my quiet place with someone, and that must be the reason that tonight you got to hear my history. Sitting here in the beautiful moonlight surrounded by the sparkling waters is different. I guess it makes a person open up. But, now you know the story of me. Quiet Dora, the loner."

He grinned then laughed as his gaze went up to the moonlight. "I think that I, for some reason have been honored that you shared all that with me. You Dora, Melvina Eldora, are entertaining." Amazing actually, but he didn't say that.

"Well," she said, softly, "I'm striving to step out a little more and for some reason I did tonight. Olivia would be proud. I never really thought about always being shielded by Star Gazer Island. That my life of hunting sea shells early in the morning and in the evening, then sitting out here on this rock alone might not be all that healthy. Seems like I have enclosed myself inside my little world here." She paused then looked stern. "Friday I'm going out of town. So I may have talked a lot but you won't be seeing me for a few days and will have this rock to yourself. I need to head inside now, but it's been nice talking to you. I hope you enjoy the rest of your evening."

With that she stood up and climbed easily down the rock like a pro. Once on the ground she gave a little wave then quickly walked along the moonlit beach toward her small house.

He just sat there, then to himself he said, "Yeah, I'll be gone the next few days too." She wasn't there to hear his words. But, when he got back maybe she'd be back here and they'd have another meeting under the moonlight.

He smiled, liking that thought. Liking it a lot.

CHAPTER SIX

Friday morning Dora experienced something strange when she didn't go to work but instead drove over to where the ranch's airstrip was located. She saw her sister's silver, two-door convertible Porsche. Kat loved her sporty car because it got her where she wanted to go and had only room for her and her bags, making it perfect. On this trip she probably didn't even bring a bag because her condo had everything she needed while there. Her favorite place, Kona.

Dora on the other hand hadn't had much idea what to pack since she traveled so little. She hopped out of her SUV, popped open the back door and pulled out her rarely used suitcase. It thumped to the ground.

"You're here, I'm so excited." Kat came rushing

over, grabbed the handle of the suitcase, taking control of it as if thinking if she pulled it to the private jet, Dora couldn't back out. Yes their dad had a private jet and also a private plane on call when needed. He had special pilots that he trusted. Even with all of that available, Dora still didn't really fly that much. Even with private jet access she was a homebody.

Kat looked over her shoulder. "Come on, walk this way. We have to get on the plane, your ride is going to be great. You know you can do it."

Dora did suffer some claustrophobia but forced one foot forward then the other. Determination had her moving over to where the pilot was waiting to help her up the stairs. He smiled and placed a hand under her elbow. "Are you okay? Kat said we were to leave as soon as you boarded."

Kat wasn't wasting time giving her a chance to back out. "Thank you, I'm fine, they just worry about me."

"Relax, we'll get you there safely."

The co-pilot was already in the seat and waved through the open door. "Great to see you. We promise to drive carefully."

"Sounds great," she said, determined and ready. She buckled her seatbelt in the front seat.

Kat sat down on the seat across the aisle. Her

computer was already sitting on a rack waiting on her. "Okay, here we go. This is going to be a long flight but a great time."

"I'm ready." And she was, she'd brought a couple of books and had thoughts rolling about what she was going to see and do when they reached the island. And she'd brought her Benadryl allergy medicine so that if she needed to, she could take it and maybe get two hours sleep. A straight two hours of sleep was good for her. She hadn't told her neighbor that sleep was something she didn't do much of and there were times that she would be sitting on that rock at all hours of the night. Just her and soft waves, sea breeze, and moonlight. Sometimes late at night or early, early in the morning because sleep evaded her often. Last night was one of those nights. She'd actually wanted to go out there but was afraid she'd see Hawk. And she didn't need to see him. Didn't need to feed this pull that she had when she was around him. These five days away would help with that.

She looked over at Kat who was watching her. "Maybe you'll take a nap on this trip. Sleep would be good. Get you ready to have fun. One day, maybe that mind of yours will slow down and let you sleep a little more."

Dora laughed, it was as if she'd been reading her

mind. "Maybe."

Kat placed a hand on hers, making Dora realize she was gripping the armrest. "It's going to be a great ride and a fun time. Yes, I have some work to do but you'll love it."

The plane was moving and off they flew. Dora was ready.

* * *

Kat was relieved that she'd gotten Dora on the plane. She and Pearl worried about Dora always staying home. They both loved to travel and seeing the world, they were workers who both got joy from what they did and it got them away from their hometown of Star Gazer. Oh, Star Gazer Island was a wonderful place and they loved it. But there was more to the world than just there. And Dora, their sweet sister, loved it. Or, as they worried and so had Olivia worried that deep down, Dora was just afraid to step out from where she felt safe.

And there was nothing wrong with feeling safe. They just knew there was a world ready for her to enjoy and if careful, keeping their guard up at all times they could see it and enjoy it. And so could Dora. And they both knew that getting her out was one of Olivia's last wishes. Their sweet friend had wished it for all of them, but both she and Pearl were not ready to settle down, so her wishes were on hold. One day, maybe. But right now, Kat loved her work and travel.

She was taking her sister on a getaway and was going to make sure Dora had a good time. But she wasn't going to spend every moment with her. She was going to give Dora space. It was time for her to explore life away from what she knew and was comfortable with. And to her there was no better place to do that than the Big Island, especially Kona. The island held a spirit she loved. Overloaded with lava that had covered the island but beauty still shined through and that was how Kat looked at life. Tragedy and sadness could and would at some time come to everyone's life in one way or the other, but she cherished the beauty of life and friendship and showed it in her restaurants. If she could feed people and make them smile it gave her peace and satisfaction. And that was what she lived for. And seeing her sister step out made her day.

The flight was faster than a commercial flight, but still almost eight hours long. Kat worked on her computer and Dora did the same. They talked and laughed in between working. The trip flew by but they were both ready to land. She'd loved seeing Dora watch out the window and see the island coming up but she was ready to get on the ground.

Flying in their dad's family jet was nice but Kat didn't always use it. She liked flying on a large plane. She would ride in first class, sit by a window and work. Normally she would fly to Hawaii in the night and sometimes sleep a little. But she'd known Dora wouldn't sleep. She had a problem with sleep but amazingly it didn't seem to interfere with her life. Dora, like others she knew about, could thrive on four hours of sleep. If she got less, then finally she would sleep and would catch up. So with that being in her mind they'd flown during daylight hours. That meant it was almost dinner time.

Dora smiled as they started their descent. "This is your favorite place isn't it?"

"Yes, it is. I love my business, my restaurants but the Big Island is my favorite. It has volcanos that are alive over on the other side. Here on this side the beauty and the peace I feel always makes me happy. My creative baking mind is working nonstop when I'm here. My condo has a great ocean view. I can stand in my kitchen and cook and bake, testing recipes while looking out the windows or sitting out on my lanai. It's a little different than Star Gazer, the water tone is just amazing.

"People love exploring the island and you'll love it too. And the fishing here is the best." She wasn't exactly sure what about the island drew her the most. People were shocked when she told them she had a restaurant in Kauai and the Big Island and might open on the other islands. But right now, she was at peace with the five restaurants that she owned. She was a busy woman keeping them all going. But had been blessed with wonderful chefs to do her work. They were happy to recreate her creations and the reviews were fantastic. That was what she looked for.

The wonderful Star Gazer Inn, whose chefs could draw people with their talent. People came from all over to see the inn and enjoy the food. Their reviews were outstanding. Her restaurant and the inn had different looks and appeal but both drew tourists and locals. Star Gazer had wonderful flower gardens and a gazebo for weddings and other gatherings. While she always got creative with things like her stairs to dinner along the river opening up to the ocean. Or like here at Kona, it was about the closeness of the ocean and the rocks, the soft lighting and the music all topped off with her tasty dishes. Restaurants weren't just about the food but the atmosphere and that was something she loved creating.

In Kona, she also had a bar for those who enjoyed a cocktail or for people alone who loved to come in and have a meal without taking a table. Or for people to gather before dinner and after to visit as they watched the sunset or the lighted water rolling in over the lava rocks surrounding them.

She looked at her sweet sister, overcome with joy. "Dora, you're going to love this. I promise. I'm so glad you came with me."

Dora smiled and her blue eyes dug into Kat's with excitement that Kat loved seeing. "I am too and I'm relaxed. I have no idea why I get anxious before flying but I'm glad we're doing this."

"That's my girl. If you traveled more it would get easier. You need to travel more, see the world."

Dora chuckled. "You and Pearl are the travelers. I'm content where I am, but y'all are right. I'm just there and happy. But stretching things a bit is good. And well..." She paused. "Girlfriend..."

"What, girlfriend?" Kat asked as they both laughed at the way they said "girlfriend". It was a joke that had come from Olivia and they carried it on.

"It was Olivia who also told me to put myself out there more. I haven't done that, so this is my new start. I'm going to try going more, stretching myself. I can't promise it, but you might get bored with me if I came with you all the time so don't worry. I sat up last night thinking about it and actually wrote down places I might like to visit. This is one of them because you love it. Watching you catch a big fish will make me smile."

"That is a wonderful plan. Me, I plan to catch

something huge tomorrow. If not, whatever comes my way I'll catch and test new recipes the following day. Tonight we'll go have dinner at the restaurant then tomorrow the fun begins, fishing is the best."

"Sounds like a great plan," Dora agreed. "Have you checked out the ranches on the island?"

"Yes, that's where I get my steaks for the restaurant. They're incredible but we have a ranch, and cowboys galore in Star Gazer, so I'm not really interested in spending a lot of time on ranches or with cowboys here on my island. I'm all about island atmosphere here. And testing new dishes and seeing the customers from all over and their reactions to my meals. That tells me a lot about the new dishes I'm trying out."

"That's what I thought. You're here but holed up cooking or working at the restaurant. Do you ever explore?"

"As in fishing in the deep blue waters, yes I do. When I first came to the island I explored the island like you're going to do. It's a fun and beautiful thing to do."

The plane started its decent and they looked out the window as the captain told them they'd be landing soon, smoothly. And they were. Her blue Jeep was waiting and she was excited as Dora's bag was loaded and they strapped into their seatbelts. Kat loved flying but loved driving more. Her Jeep was open and let the air swirl around them, giving her a feeling of freedom as they drove from the airport toward the main road. Lava rock was everywhere along the way, but still, this was the place she adored. She was home…

Yes, Kat called this home, to herself anyway. She did love the island and hoped Dora did too.

"That's a lot of boats," Dora said as they passed the marina.

Yes, it is. Fishermen love fishing here in this great place. There are many kinds but they love to catch the Marlins like I do. If they don't catch it they usually at least feel it on their hook and that gives them the want to come back and try again."

Dora leaned back and took a deep breath as the air sent her long golden hair swirling. That made Kat happy. She reached out and touched her sister's arm. "We're going to have a great time."

Yes, they were.

CHAPTER SEVEN

They arrived at Kat's condo, it was beautiful, with a wide window and doors that opened onto a large patio, exactly like her sister described it. Dinner at her restaurant sounded great and they jumped back in the Jeep and drove through the pretty town, past several stores and restaurants and then to the Cafe By The Seaside. The Hawaiian music drifted outside through the large open windows. Dora loved the feeling and was impressed with the beautiful atmosphere. Yes, she'd seen photos but the instant cozy, fun, and elegant feeling all in one was fantastic. She could see across the bay a beautiful hotel and Kat told her that was where they'd go for breakfast in the morning because it was a lovely place.

"Sounds great but right now I'm looking forward to dinner here."

"Me too."

They entered the restaurant and headed to the bar area near the water's edge as smiling waiters and waitresses greeted Kat warmly. The door to the kitchen was near the back of the bar area and instantly a group came through the door.

"Chef Ridge," Kat said, giving the small man a hug as he threw his arms open.

"Boss, it's great to have you back," he said, grinning huge as he patted Kat on the back. "I was getting tired and need a break so it's great to have you here."

Everyone surrounding them from the kitchen and the customers laughed.

Kat gave the grinning man a hug. "You work so hard, I'll for sure give you some relief." It was obviously a joke, she loved it. Her sister had a special way about her when it came to running her businesses and her employees enjoyed it.

"You know you can't run me out of the kitchen," he said then looked at Dora and hitched a brow. "You do know that no one can outwork or out cook your sister."

"I know it. She was in the kitchen by the age of five

and I was barely old enough to remember at two years old but I do. Mom had to learn to give her space to create and me and Pearl were her test bunnies.

He grinned. "Was it good then?"

"Not always. But shortly thereafter, we began commissioning her work."

He nodded. "That's what I thought. Her mind is always generating wonderful culinary ideas."

"He's a great chef too," Kat said. "So is my other chef, Tess. They can't be beat."

"Okay have a seat," Kat said, patting the bar seat. "Sit here, and I'll be back.

Dora took a seat at the bar and looked around the room. It was packed but like many resorts it had no real walls, just a large area with the indoor seating then a huge area out in the open and on the stoned area by the water. Every table was packed. Then Kat and her crew disappeared into the kitchen. Dora ordered a water with lemon, leaned back in the chair and enjoyed the music and the sparkling lights glistening on the low tide of water rolling in. Her sister knew how to choose the right spots for her restaurants.

Soon Kat came back outside carrying two amazing-looking plates of fresh shrimp and lobster. "Couldn't help but grab our favorites." She sat the plates down, then slid onto her bar stool. "This is going to be great."

Dora smiled at her. "Thanks for getting me here, sis. I'm glad I came."

Kat grinned. "Awesome. That's what I wanted to hear."

And then they dug into their dinner and she knew instantly why her sister's restaurants were so sought after.

The next morning they got up and went to Don's for breakfast. It was on the huge back patio of a lovely, amazing hotel that was right on the water. The ocean and lava rocks surrounded the dining area and the table they got was right by the low stone wall. It was beautiful and peaceful and the breakfast was fantastic. She chose a bowl of fresh fruit and couldn't resist the French toast. While they ate they watched the huge ships out on the horizon and smaller fishing boats heading across the bay and out to fish. Soon they joined them.

And within an hour of thinking that, they were loaded onto their chartered fishing boat and headed out. The boat was beautiful and large for just the two of them and the three men there to get them out to where they located the fish. It wasn't even an hour later when something caught the hook of the large pole and line and like she knew exactly what she was doing Kat had the large reel and took her seat in the large padded chair that was attached solidly to the boat and the fishing began.

The driver did his thing, keeping the boat where it needed to be as Kat reeled in, and worked the line slowly but surely bringing the large Blue Marlin closer to the boat. It was amazing to see her sister's muscles working as she, like the professional fisherman she obviously could be, reeled the huge Marlin closer.

Thrilled for her sister, Dora grabbed onto the metal ladder that led up to the seat high above the deck and from there she started taking a video. She'd done the climb as if she were climbing the large rock in her own cove and was as comfortable there as she was on her rock.

She was startled and happy when she realized how good her sister was at fishing and that Dora climbed up and recorded it. She also got a snap of the startled look on Kat's face when she found her high above her. Dora snapped a picture of that look to have for always. Maybe startling her family would be fun.

She laughed, her laugh would be on the tape too, and her sister would always know that behind the scenes, she'd been there enjoying watching her fish on the deep waters off the coast of Kailua-Kona. She was glad she'd come. Later as they eased back into the boat docking area she'd had a blast. She so enjoyed the crew and the way they'd helped Kat do what she loved to do. But she was glad they weren't going out tomorrow. As they were out on the water she could see the coastline and that was what she enjoyed. And tomorrow she would be the one driving while her sister stayed home and cooked. It would be her day to get out alone doing her thing and if she needed her sister at any time she was a phone call away. Dora smiled at Kat's words. Yes, she was an adult and could handle any problems that came her way but she told Kat she'd call if she needed her but not to wait on the call.

When they got inside they sat out on the porch listening to music drifting in from the restaurants down the road and they'd enjoyed the sunset. They'd eaten a good meal, an easy meal. Tomorrow would be Kat's experiment cooking day and she could tell as they sat there on the balcony that Kat's brain was already working.

Hers was too, and an excitement filled her. She might like traveling after all.

* * *

The next morning Dora was ready to explore. She was looking forward to driving toward the head of the island where there was a beautiful golf course surrounded by homes and a great beach and restaurant. Kat had told her that on the beach she would see sea turtles and maybe sea shells. That had her wanting to go.

If she got adventurous, she could get in the water but that was a joke, Dora didn't swim in the ocean. Never had, she preferred searching the sand on shore. She had her sun dress on, her flip-flops, and a hat. After a quick breakfast, she dropped Kat off at her condo, and then she was on the road, alone, on an adventure.

This was her day. And she felt free, and felt Olivia smiling.

Amazing, oh so amazing.

She drove along the road toward Kawaihae, lava rocks all along the way, as she watched for the sign to the beach where she was heading. She could see cattle sometimes, out in the pastures and knew that there were many ranches out this way. It wasn't the look of a Texas ranch, but it intrigued her. No, she didn't work on their ranch, but she loved it. She'd always thought that if she ever did find a man to marry he had to be a cowboy.

She was here in Hawaii thinking about cowboys. Or the cowboy she might find and marry one day, if she got the nerve up to do it. Her problem was worrying about being where her poor brother had been. Could she love and lose? The thought rushed through Dora as Olivia took the seat in the Jeep beside her. Not really, but in that moment she felt her friend, and heard her telling her yes she could do it. That love was worth it even if for a short time.

Dora looked toward the passenger's seat but it was empty, no matter how much it felt like her friend had really been there beside her.

"Have fun," Dora said, feeling the wind blowing her hair into chaos and her hands gripping the steering wheel as she felt freedom sweep around her. She focused on that. She had no deadline. No stress and that was her plan. Not getting dragged into sorrow.

She turned into the opening leading to the area where the homes, golf course and restaurants were. It was the beach she was looking for, to explore and she saw it, long, full of lava rocks and gentle waves. She sighed, it was time to walk and explore.

Dora climbed from the Jeep in the large parking lot. She had on her sandals that could handle sand and instead of heading for the area where the beach and restaurant were, she went to the left. She headed across a sand dune and headed away from what looked like a full beach area of everyone enjoying the sun. As she topped the hill she smiled at the coastline of black lava rock with blue water wandering in through it to the sandy shore. And instantly she spotted her first sea turtle lying on a flat rock as if enjoying the sunshine more than anyone. She headed down the hill and then took a picture of the turtle, glancing into the sand for sea shells.

WHAT'S LOVE GOT TO DO WITH IT

She saw none there that caught her eyes.

Others were walking the beach and looking at the various turtles on various lava rocks. She watched for special sea shells and found a few before rounding a turn and saw a young couple sitting on a rock kissing. She smiled as she kept on walking. Nice. She wasn't looking for an attraction but loved it when people found it like her brother had, twice. For some odd reason as she passed by the couple her thoughts went to her neighbor and she wondered what he was doing and where he had traveled to.

She'd made sure to avoid going out to her rock in case he might be there again, but as she stopped to look at two large turtles resting on the rocks, she wondered if his view was as good as hers.

She took a deep breath as the rolling waves washed in over the lava rock and the sand in between. As she stood there a new turtle came swimming in. Fewer people were this far down and she liked it. But her stomach growled and she realized it was time for lunch.

Though she'd picked up a few shells, she'd found nothing spectacular. The shells were in her big pocket bulging on her right side. She was sure many tourists looked this way after walking on the beach, so she headed back toward the dining area. Then when she reached it she told the young lady she'd like a beach view if one was available.

"I'm Lettie, your host, and have a few that might work. Would you rather be in the shade or does it matter?"

"Either works for me, Lettie. As long as I have the view."

Lettie smiled. "Then you've got it. Most take the shade so you get my favorite table at the far edge and in the bright sunlight. I'm like you. I love the sun, I wear my sunscreen and my shades and I'm good. Now if I had light skin, it might not be so easy. My friend sunburns just by breathing the sun's heat."

Dora liked her. She was talkative and entertaining as she led her to the table. Her sister would really like her, just what Kat loved about hiring people. Personality that was nice and entertaining while on target but non-intrusive.

"Here you go, does it work?"

"Yes, wonderful." They were on the edge of the stone dining area and the sun shined on her table and the empty one next to it.

"Great. Your waitress will be by soon."

Dora watched Lettie walk away and then sat down. It was a quiet spot with a view. She could see the other diners, then to the other side of the beach and that was where her gaze stayed.

Then she heard Lettie's voice coming back and a male voice interacting with her. Instantly Dora looked their way and was shocked as a tall cowboy walked with Lettie to the table beside hers. He was her neighbor.

Hawk looked from the hostess to her and shock lit his face as much as shock was racing through her.

"Dora." He smiled. "You're in Kona also?"

Her lips spread upward in an unstoppable smile. Then she laughed. "I am. This is where my sister's restaurant is and her favorite place. I'd never been and I told you I was going on a trip. And you were going on a trip too. And here we are."

"Yes, here." They stared at each other smiling and a tingling sensation washed through Dora.

"Would you like to sit together?" Lettie asked, a smile in the sound of her voice.

Hawk hitched a brow. "Would you like a visitor?"

"Sure, that would be great."

The grinning Lettie laid his menu on her table. "So you two act like you know each other well, but didn't know you were both coming to Kona? And, are you from Texas? I think that's what I hear."

Dora chuckled. "Yes, I have a Texas twang that is real. And we both live at Star Gazer Island in Texas."

The girl's eyes widened. "You live at the same place that Kat McConnell, the owner of the restaurant in

Kona lives?"

Dora's alerts went up. "Yes, she's my sister."

"I heard wonderful things about the restaurant and have been thinking about applying for a waitress job there in Kona or a hostess job. And maybe one day work at Star Gazer Island. She and her restaurants have a wonderful reputation and I love my job. Most people would say why do you love being a waitress but I do. I meet so many people from all over, like you two. But also, the restaurant has such a great reputation that I'd love to work there."

Dora grinned. "You give me your name and number and I'll give it to my sister with a great review. Just the way you greeted me and brought me to this table. The smile on your face, your communication skills put me at ease instantly. My sister would love having you in her restaurant if she has any openings. That I don't know, but she looks for people with attitudes like yours."

"Thank you very much. I'll give you the info before you leave, but I'll let you two have a great lunch now. Your waitress will be right over."

"You're the one who has been very accommodating and has me looking forward to the meal."

They smiled and then Lettie walked away. Then Dora looked across the table at her neighbor. "Who would have thought I'd find you here in the middle of Kona by the sea? I can't believe it that we both came here at the same time."

"It's odd. We flew half a world away and here we are."

"Yes, I know why I'm here, with my sister taking some time off. What about you, are you taking time off too?"

"I own a house that my crew has been finishing up on, I came for a last look before I put it on the market."

"Seriously. You even buy homes to remodel in Hawaii."

Hawk chuckled. "I have wanderlust in my blood. I can't help it. I love to travel and see things and doing business like that makes it work for me. I'm a single guy with nothing tying me down."

They stared at each other and her heart thundered as lightning struck inside her chest and suddenly she didn't care. She liked looking at him. She liked him. This was not a normal situation. It was great.

As if it was meant to be.

CHAPTER EIGHT

Still reeling from the surprise he'd felt the moment he saw Dora, Hawk stared at the beautiful woman sitting across the table from him. She looked as disbelieving as he felt.

"You're actually remodeling a house here?" she asked.

"Yes, a little mind-blowing that we should be at the same place at the same time across the ocean from home."

"Crazy is what it is. You buy property everywhere?"

"A lot of places. I have a house here on the golf course that my men have just finished renovating. It's a beautiful place that I'd thought about living in myself.

But that would have meant longer trips than I wanted to do. Then I went to an art show of Nina McIntyre and met her and Jackson. That lady is a true artist. I loved the painting of the cattle on the ranch with a stunning sunset. When she told me it was from their own property a short drive from Star Gazer Island we started talking. I bought the painting then came to the Island and I was sold instantly on it. I like it so much that I decided to live there and use it as my headquarters for a while."

He was thankful he'd done that because he'd met his neighbor. The small woman with a smile that did things to his insides. Her gaze was on him now, the woman had eyes that would give the water off the coast of Kona a challenge, their tone sparkled in the sunlight. His brain was working overtime but he couldn't rein it in. This couldn't be an accident.

"I was coming for lunch then heading back to town. I fly out tomorrow for another meeting in Houston on Monday."

"It's odd isn't it."

"Yes, very," he agreed. "But, I'm liking it." And he was, couldn't help it.

The waitress brought their ice water, smiled. "I'll be back in a few moments to take your order." Then she walked away, obviously not wanting to intrude on their conversation.

Hawk was glad she gave him and Dora time to talk. "Did you fly into the airport in Kona?"

"Yes, we used Dad's private jet, he insisted."

"That's nice. Kat comes here a lot?"

"Yes, she has a lovely condo in Kona and loves it. I'm liking it too. After we dropped our things off we went to her restaurant on the bay and had an amazing meal. Yesterday we went out fishing, she caught a Blue Marlin and I took pictures and fishing might be good for me because last night I actually slept good. Something I'm not the best at doing."

"Might have been the rocking motion from being on the boat. It can stay with you for a while."

"That might have been what it was."

"I'm glad something helped you sleep."

"Me too," she said, sighing. "I'm used to not sleeping though. But something was different, because I'm not a good sleeper. But when I've had several days of light sleep *or* no sleep at all, I'll finally sleep better. Not great, but enough. *Last* night was the best that I remember in a while, a very long time."

"Maybe you should go fishing more often." He grinned and she laughed.

"Maybe. There are a lot of maybe's in this conversation."

He laughed. "Maybe, but I'm enjoying it."

"Me too. I guess we better look at the menu. I had a great breakfast at Don's Mai Tai Bar & Restaurant overlooking Kailua Bay, but it's worn off. Have you been there? It has a great view of the ocean like this but even closer and a wonderful breakfast menu."

"It is a great place. I'm actually staying there," Hawk said. "I must have eaten earlier than you and Kat. Speaking of Kat, where is she?"

"She's testing recipes. Kat's obsessed and loves it here because she also loves fishing. We were raised on a ranch and can ride horses with the best of them, but oddly all of us girls are not doing anything that has to do with ranching. After seeing her out there on that boat yesterday, I could see her someday living here or spending more time here on Kona."

"She loves it that much?"

"She does, but what do I know? The woman stays really busy. I mean, she even loves to fish." She laughed. "But, she seems more relaxed here than I've ever seen her. I even think she could start fishing and selling it to all the restaurants, she loves it that much. She really fits in."

He liked Dora's way of talking, she was quiet but when she got excited she beamed, and she obviously loved her sister because she was beaming brightly. "Kona's not my favorite place, but meeting you here has pushed this little island to the top."

She blushed at his words that he *probably* shouldn't have said, but he did anyway. Her eyes flicked across his face and he had the sudden urge to be closer to her. To hold her in his arms, to kiss her—the thought was a sucker punch. He needed to back up. This was the first time in a very long time he'd thought that. *Business* was what he thought about. But, right now he could care less about work.

Their waitress came back. "Would you like me to take your order now? Lettie told me you two were from the same town in Texas and ran into each other here. Told me not to interrupt you too much but I figured you might want to order."

He looked back at Dora. "The barbeque is great here. Had it yesterday with my crew."

"Really, you are in Hawaii and you're eating barbeque."

"They raise great beef here."

She looked at the waitress. "Then I'll take what he's having. Test it against Texas barbeque."

"I'll take the beef brisket and the potato salad and the key lime pie and she'll have the same."

"You won't be sorry," the waitress said looking at Dora before she walked away.

They smiled at each other. Dora placed her palm on

the table. "This is slightly odd."

He nodded. "Yes, we both traveled this far and then meet up again. I'll say that I did go sit on your rock again, hoping to talk some more. But you didn't come out. I got to thinking I might be keeping you away from it so haven't been back. And then I find you here."

"I was getting ready for the trip so I was busy…honestly, I've never sat on that rock with anyone before. So, I was a bit confused. It's my place to be alone."

"You like to spend time alone."

"I'm comfortable that way. But I enjoyed sitting there on the rock with you. I just didn't want to, you know, get… used to it."

"We're neighbors, but honestly, don't worry. I'm here eating with you now because we're here. But you don't have to… okay I won't lie. I'm not a man who lets myself get interested in a woman. I tried not to be, but goodness we're half a world away and here we are. Me denying that I'm not interested would be a flat-out lie. And I'm not a lying man."

She blushed again and those eyes twinkled like diamonds then she chuckled. "Then I'll admit it too. I'm not one to normally say that, but yes, I like you. And this does put a twist on us being neighbors."

He liked this lady. "Now that we have that out in the open, we'll take this nice and slow like neighbors should. Believe me, I don't want to mess up the friendship we've made."

"I appreciate that," she said, and then they talked. They talked about the house he was working on.

"If you'd like to see it I can take you there after we eat."

Lunch was served and they talked, he enjoyed every moment. Then he paid, insisted on it and she got Lettie's info and stood up. He laughed when he saw that one of her pockets was full.

"What is that?" he asked, grinning.

"I have a pocket full of sea shells. I didn't find that many but I loved seeing all the sea turtles resting on the rocks."

"There is a great place I could take you to that might have a lot more shells. It's not too far down the road if you want to or have time after you look at the house."

"That would be great. I have the entire day. Kat is working at home then going to the restaurant tonight. I'll probably go to her home and change then go there for dinner. Honestly, I think she wanted me to have the whole day to myself. She and Pearl are trying to get me to be more adventurous."

"Well then, Darl'n—Dora," he corrected his words but felt the *Darl'n* race through him. She was a darling lady and he wanted to spend time with her. "We'll go for a ride and see the cove I'm talking about."

WHAT'S LOVE GOT TO DO WITH IT

She smiled and his insides rumbled, this was a great moment. He just had to be careful.

* * *

After they went to the home on the golf course he'd renovated, Dora was stunned once again by the man's ability, his obvious talent and most of all his span of jobs. "You bought this all the way from Texas and then remodeled it from nice to outstanding. It's beautiful."

"Thanks, and yes I did."

"You and my sister-in-law Kelley would get along great. She does the houses with glass everywhere."

She looked at him, her heart stumbled so her gaze went back where it needed to be, scanning the sliding glass wall that went from floor to ceiling. She walked to the door and he beat her to it, slid it open and let her walk out onto the large patio that stretched wide, overlooking the beautiful golf course. A golf course that also had the distracting bay as a backdrop for many golfers and obvious home buyers. Which had brought Hawk here to this spot.

Palm trees and sand traps dotted the golf greens. She could see happy men and women out there having a great time. Golf lovers everywhere.

She turned and found him leaning against the thick, varnished porch post that glowed like a work of art as did the other six that ran down the large patio. He looked relaxed and was concentrating on her, not the scenery—her thoughts stumbled...

He cocked his head. "I find good buys and if it draws me I go look and then see the area around it. If the home and land have potential then I make an offer. Like I said, I was thinking about being here in Hawaii for a short time so I came, saw it, liked it, and had plans. But *then* while I was back in Texas, I went to the art show by Nina, the artist everyone is raving about and I met Nina and her husband Jackson. They talked about Star Gazer Island and their ranch that was near there and where that painting was inspired and I decided to go look. And I am so glad I did."

Dora's insides trembled. "I'm glad you're my neighbor, not sure how long you'll be there with that drive in you to see new places, to explore. Now you're stuck there in Star Gazer Island but still odd to find you here. My sister will be shocked also when she finds out."

"She comes here often?"

"As often as possible. She is a roamer. She loves the area. She has another one in Kauai and then three in Texas, one in Galveston, the one in Star Gazer, and one in Corpus Christi. She loves her business."

"Sounds like it."

"She stays really busy and loves it. I don't think she

will and I'm hoping she doesn't, open another one until a place really inspires her. She's overworked I think. But that's just me, the gal who starts her day off wandering along the beach and ends it the same way."

He smiled at her words. "I think that's great. You seem at peace."

Peace. "I'm… I'm looking for it." She wasn't there at the moment as she and Hawk held gazes. Could she find peace like Olivia had if she let herself open her heart? She'd never felt so drawn to do so as she did in that moment standing a few steps from Hawk. She needed to get her mind off of where it had gone. "Have you not eaten at one of Kat's restaurants?"

"No, I haven't. I eat at Star Gazer Inn, and it's amazing but I'll have to try it out."

"Yes, you will. If you're not tired of my company after we look at the beach, I'll meet you at the one in Kona and you can try it out." She had stepped off a cliff.

He grinned, pulled himself away from the post. "That sounds like a deal I can't turn down. You have a date—a dinner partner."

She laughed, truly laughed. "You're as skeptical of dating as I am."

"Not because I'm scared of you but because I'm scared of… doing something wrong." Hawk stood there on the beautiful porch and knew he'd made the right move taking the house in Star Gazer Island instead of this one. He was going to make the one he lived in the best remodel he'd ever done. "Do you think your sister-in-law might help me design a glass ceiling in my home in Star Gazer?"

"I'm sure she would love to do that. She's very busy."

"I'm sure she is and I completely understand if she doesn't have time."

"She'll have time to talk to you and then y'all can work that out. I'll just introduce you." She felt confident that Kelley would be glad to talk to Hawk.

"Thank you. The house has great potential and I'm sure you've seen that too if you've looked at it."

"Yes, I saw it, but not since Kelley came into our lives and seeing her vision of glass and open space in homes. So, now you've put that in my mind about the home you've bought and I'm intrigued."

"And that makes it all the better for me to create what I'm seeing." He smiled and she felt it to her toes. "Now, let's go look for some sea shells."

"Sounds like a great plan." She quickly passed through the door he was waiting for her to go through. She brushed his arm in passing with her arm and knew that she might be in trouble. A mere brushing of arms sent her off level ground.

And she didn't mind the erratic way her heart was now playing in her chest.

CHAPTER NINE

They got into Hawk's large Jeep, it had its top off so the wind swirled around them as he drove down the road, the water in the distance across the lava-covered land. Then they rounded a huge bend in the road, the ocean was closer and down below them. A huge stretch of high land stood out in the water and the waves could be seen rolling into the area and in some places spraying into the air.

"It's beautiful," she gasped. Star Gazer did not have this.

"I thought you'd like it. You can't see it but there is a small beach area." He turned onto a dirt road that wound down through the rocky area and out of view from the road they'd been on. She was sitting up in her seat watching their descent and then he brought the Jeep to a halt on the side of the dirt road. "It's walking from here on down." He pulled a bag from the back of the Jeep. "For your shells. We'll use it instead of your pockets."

"Much better. Thank you. It looks like a great walk." She started down the trail.

"When we get to the beach hopefully you'll find some sea shells. Though they do have restrictions."

"I won't take many. Just a few unique ones if I find some. I have plenty of sea shells on my beach."

"You know I have some shells on my beach if you ever come around the end of the rock."

"I've done that a few times before you bought, but not since."

"Come around that rock any time you want to."

"Same for you," she said, pausing.

Hawk moved a step ahead of her, then he started walking, leading the way and feeling better being in front in case she slipped. When they reached the bottom of the trail he waited for her.

"There on top of that huge rock right there is probably a wonderful place to watch the sunset." Hands on hips she stared ahead at the rock.

"It might be. But I won't be here tomorrow and we'd have to sit here a long time tonight to see it, then miss dinner. Maybe after we get home you'll meet me out on our rock. Your rock."

"I think that sounds like a great plan." And she did. She was on an adventure, stepping out of her closed-in closet and this trip helped. it was as if Hawk had been dropped in on this adventure and she was glad. Hopefully there would be no regrets. Regrets was where she didn't want to go. Out of anything, she was quiet, dated a few times and had been dropped and never let that happen again. She was the dropper but then the non-dater after losing Olivia.

Dating hadn't appealed to her at all since the loss of her sister-in-law, her friend. Loving someone, losing them, no, she might be being adventurous right now but she wasn't sure how far she could go. Hawk was a handsome, kind, and intriguing man but she wasn't sure how much of a risk she could take. Then it slammed into her that she'd just thought about it. And about him.

And that as an adult was the first time she'd ever thought anything like that. She'd never felt drawn to any man enough to think about crossing that line of friendship and love… until now.

* * *

Hawk was thankful when they reached the beach. It was

a very steep incline to a small beach. On his first and only trip until now, he hadn't seen anyone take the walk down to the sand. On his first trip he'd come here because he'd been told it was beautiful and he'd walked down here alone and sat on a rock and watched the waves rush in. They'd rushed in so hard that he'd been splashed by a big one slamming against the rocks. He had a feeling she would laugh too if that happened.

They reached the water's edge and Dora slipped her feet from her sandals. "It's take off the shoes time."

"Sounds good." He laughed, sat on a rock not caring if it was wet, then tugged each of his boots and socks off. As she watched he rolled his jeans to his calves and stood up as her dress skirt floated up in the wind and like a pro she snagged it with her fingers, twisted one edge and tied it in a knot right above her knees.

"There, no more floating in the wind."

He held out his hand to her. "I think you've done that before."

"A few times back home." She looked at his hand.

"This water is rougher than back home," he said and she slipped her hand into his.

"Let's do this together then. If one of us stumbles the other one can go down too, or together stay upright." She laughed. "I don't think I can hold you up."

"I'm ready to be the hero. If you start to go down I'll sweep you up, save you from the vicious water."

She laughed. "I'm suddenly feeling adventurous, and probably would never say this again but I might slip on purpose now."

His grin widened. "That sounds like a great deal."

* * *

She chuckled then moved forward, needing space and not planning on tripping. At least not on purpose no matter how enticing it suddenly was to her.

Searching the stunning topaz water now swirling around her feet she loved the moment, walking in the water with this man at her side. His hand holding hers in a secure way.

For distraction she looked out to sea. Star Gazer Island's water wasn't as blue as this. Then in the incoming wave she spotted the black spread-out kite wings of a large stingray with a white dotted body. "Look, a stingray. Two," she said as another one came in to view. Together they rode the wave, gliding with it and the sun beaming through the water and over them.

"Beautiful," Dora gasped. "They know how to ride those waves like they're part of it."

"It's stunning," Hawk said. "But, now it's time to

step out of the water and walk onto the beach just in case one we can't see is hiding beneath the sandy water. The last thing I'd want to happen is for you to get stung."

"Right, that sounds good," she said as they backed up onto the sand away from the water rolling. "Just so you know, on Star Gazer you have to watch too, not that it happens often but it does."

They started walking down the beach line and she saw a sparkle, pulling her hand from Hawk's she hurried toward the shining shell. She bent down and picked it up but it wasn't a shell, it was a large pink glass starfish. It was beautiful.

"Look at this. Amazing. It must have been someone's special buy from a store and they lost it and now it's mine." Then she spotted a blue rock of glass glistening in the sand. She picked it up too and held them in her hands. "If you would pick up those two sea shells," she said, nodding toward two sandy shapes leaning against each other. "I'll have my shells. I'll always wonder who these belonged to and how they lost it. This is my souvenir."

He picked up the shells. "I haven't made it into your gift store but I'll be there soon. You have an eye for beauty and things with special meanings. I have a feeling your store shows that. And your home too, probably. Will you create something with these?"

His words touched her, because she prided herself in special things. Things that would touch people of all price ranges but all affordable to someone.

"These will be mine. My memory of our adventure today. I'll give them a glass box to live in." This truly had been her jewel of a day. Unexpected few hours with Hawk that she would never forget.

"That sounds great. I'll have to find some now for my memory."

She spotted a large shell that cleaned up could sit alone and be nice. She went over and picked it up. "How about this to sit on an office shelf or bookshelf."

Hawk took it from her, their fingers brushing. "Perfect."

Yes, it was.

CHAPTER TEN

Hawk couldn't believe the day he had had. He had followed Dora to her sister's condo and then said he would be back and pick her up in an hour and a half, which was the time that she had set up with her sister for them to come to dinner. He had heard the conversation or portions of it and had heard the tension in Dora's voice when she had had to explain that yes, she was bringing someone to eat with her and it just happened to be her neighbor from Star Gazer Island.

She'd looked at him and had smiled and given a shrug. I mean, who would've thought that they could have run into each other all across the ocean like this? Again, just the idea had him a little off-centered, but he wasn't unhappy.

Right now he was just riding the wave, couldn't help it. The woman rocked his boat even though he had lived through a tumultuous ocean or turbulent ride in every aspect of his life other than building his empire in real estate. Closing himself off the last few years from everyone suddenly seemed ridiculous at the moment. All he was going to think about was dinner with his beautiful neighbor, but it wasn't her outside beauty that drew him as much as the lady herself. She was unique and he liked how she had told him about where her and her sisters names came from and that she was like the ancestor Katie Pearl.

It was a great history, but it wasn't her history he was interested in. It was right now as he drove up his heart twisted like a tornado seeing her walk out the door. She wore a beautiful dress that looked as if it had been bought just for the island with its coral and blue ocean tones that swirled together as it flowed over her, like the gentle lady that she was. Yes, Dora was gentle.

"Hello again. You look beautiful," he said as he strode around to her side to open her door. He held his hand out and she took it and then settled onto the seat.

"Thank you. When I called and made the reservation they connected me to Kat and I told her how we met up. She was as startled as we were, and said we would have her favorite seat by the water. She's going to come out and meet you."

"I will be glad to meet her." He closed the door, then he strode around to his side of the Jeep, hopped in and off they went.

The restaurant was very close to her condo. They actually got there almost within the blink of an eye and he parked and then hopped out and went to open her door, but she was already out.

They walked into the restaurant and he was floored by its Hawaiian beauty, a walkway with candles, lights along the path, music playing, and the ocean surrounding it. You could hear it and see it through the crowd that sat on the open terrace. Her sister obviously had an eye for making things right. A gorgeous view over the black rocks and the blue water glistened in the lights that were there along the edge of a lot of the restaurants along the bay.

The minute they stepped up to the hostess, she beamed, "It's good to see you again. Welcome. Miss Kat has put you at the perfect table for you two, and she's very excited." Dora glanced at him sideways as they followed the nice waitress. Sensing Dora's uneasiness, he placed his hand at her lower back wanting to give her comfort.

The moment his fingers touched her, lightning shot through him and she glanced over her shoulder, the same shock in her eyes. She smiled and he held his hand exactly where it was as they ended up on the front row at the end on the corner. He liked it. They were out of the view of everyone who looked at the musician, but they had a view. He could care less. The only view he wanted was Dora.

He pulled her chair out then looked at the smiling hostess. "Thank you. Please tell her sister it's a beautiful view, a beautiful spot."

"Yes," Dora added. "Please tell Kat that we're here and we like the spot."

"I'll do that. Now, here's your menus and I'm sure the moment I speak to your sister, she'll be out. Have a great evening." And then she turned and walked away.

Dora sat down in the chair and then he took his seat across from her at the small table. He placed one hand on the table and looked at her. "I hope this isn't stressing you out too much. It's a beautiful place. I'm glad to get to share this with you before I fly away tomorrow." He meant it.

"It's been a great day," she said, softly then smiled. Thank goodness. The last thing he wanted to do was scare her away. "I don't know what my sister's going to think when she comes out."

He smiled as in that moment, over Dora's shoulder he saw a gorgeous lady in a teal dress coming their way.

That had to be Kat, her rusty curled hair was pulled back in a ponytail that splayed out from the curls and bounced as she strode their way. Her lean muscular arms told him that she worked out hard and strength and confidence radiated from her. They looked similar enough for him to know this was Kat. Dora was smaller and her golden blonde hair radiated her soft beauty. Her sister was tall, lean, and vivacious, while Dora was small and beautiful like the seashells she hunted.

"Hi, I'm Kat," she said the moment she reached them and instantly Dora turned to smile at her.

"I'm Hawk and glad to meet you too." He'd stood instantly and took her held out hand. She shook his hand with the vigor of a woman who knew how to show she was in control. He smiled. He liked her and knew instantly that she was sending a message that she was here to check him out and protect her sister and that made him a fan.

"I'm startled by this whole thing," Kat said letting go of him to hug Dora.

His gaze locked with Dora's. "Dora showed me how to hunt for seashells today."

They all sat back down. "It was a great day," Dora said.

Kat's expression was radiant as she smiled from Dora to him. "I can't even imagine flying all the way across the ocean and then meeting your neighbor. Sometimes things are just odd but interesting, so I'm glad you're here and you're going to eat at my restaurant."

He nodded. "Dora said that you have a lot of restaurants and that you really like this one and that you like to fish."

"I love to fish. I'm a rancher's daughter like Dora, but Dora is great on a horse and in picking great heifers for the ranch. Plus, her art at making treasures out of seashells makes her the best at everything, but cooking." Kat grinned. "I got the cooking talent and she got everything else."

Hawk zeroed in on Kat's praise of her sister. He looked at Dora. "So you're great on a horse and in picking heifers?"

Kat butted in. "This gal is a dynamo on a horse and used to help Dad wrangle them until she opened her beautiful treasure store."

"I don't talk about it much either, but I can ride, enjoy it."

"So, when I buy a new horse for my place we can take a ride?"

"You're buying a horse?" Dora looked shocked.

"I ride. I just sold my horses because I was traveling so much, after I get my horse delivered we can take a ride."

"That's a great idea." Kat beamed at her sister.

"Your horse is getting delivered?" Dora looked stunned.

"It's been at a trainer. I'm going to have him delivered next week. I think he's coming in on Thursday. He's a great horse, Dora. We may have to go for a ride."

"Sure, that sounds great. I do love riding. I just knew I wasn't going to always be a cowgirl. I have this thing about seashells and that's what drew me to this."

Woman. There was something about her. One moment she was vibrant. One moment she was quiet. It was hard to completely figure her out, and of course there was no reason. They were just friends. Well, he was completely drawn to her and wasn't completely sure what to do about it. That kept repeating through him that her sudden quietness here in front of her sister was different than when it had just been him and her.

Kat stood up. "Well, I'm going to leave you two alone. Y'all are neighbors, so y'all need to get to know each other a little bit better and you pick out what you want. We have wonderful food and it's so fresh here and so wonderful and I'll bring you a little something that I worked on today. I'll have them deliver it to you. I'm working in the kitchen. I know I'm dressed like this. It doesn't look like it, but in the back, I have a big old apron that I wear and love it, so enjoy your meal."

"You too, and I am glad that I got to meet you." She smiled at both of them and then turned and headed back.

Their waitress came instantly and brought them a bottle of water and filled the wine glasses with icy water and then asked if they wanted anything else to drink and would be glad to bring it to them. Dora said, "Lemon," and he nodded.

"For me too, please." And then she left. "Okay, so now I know your sister and I also know that you get nervous when you're around people. Is that what's going on? I mean, I don't want to make you nervous."

She looked at him. "I'm okay. I have problems sometimes. My sister is beautiful. Amazing, so talented."

"I see that, but to be honest, Dora, and point blank, it is not your sister that I'm interested in."

* * *

When dinner was finished, he wasn't ready for it to be finished. He would sit there across from this wonderful lady. Watch the sunset over and over again. It was something he could get used to. Of course, to be honest, they barely knew each other, but there were a lot of women that he barely knew, but none of them drew him to even think about having dinner with them over and over again.

He paid the bill when the sweet waitress brought it and they were finished whether he was ready or not. "This was nice. I know we said when we get back to the States, we would be friends, but I'm hoping, maybe you might let me take you out again."

Dora's eyes twinkled in the soft lights surrounding them. "I've had a great time and if I told you no, that wouldn't be nice. So, I'll say yes. I actually think that would be a great idea. Well, honestly when I came here with Kat, I just thought I would be relaxing and enjoying the sun and go fishing with her. She is the fish-loving one. I mean, me and a boat are not best friends even though I have lived on the coast all my life."

"You are a seashell hunter, not a fisherman." He liked the way her eyes lit up again as her lips curled up in a soft smile.

"Yes, going hunting for seashells is my odd love. And thank you for taking me where we went today, it was great. And tonight has been wonderful also. So yes, I would enjoy going to dinner with you in our normal environment."

"Great—"

"But honestly, if you get back and decide you don't—"

He reached across the table and covered her hand that lay temptingly beside her plate. "I want this. I want to go out to dinner with you." Touching her lit up the night for him and he had a feeling, a hope that she felt it too. "So I guess now that I've got that out of the way, I guess I need to take you back and then head back to the room. My flight leaves really early in the morning."

Dora smiled again, that beautiful smile that touched him on the inside and the outside. "I think you're right and I guess my sister must have known that we were probably getting toward the end of our meal because here she comes."

Kat walked up right then. "I know y'all are leaving, I could tell. I didn't come out earlier when I glanced out from the kitchen, but I just want to say it's so nice to meet you and I'm thrilled that you live in Star Gazer Island near our ranch. You know that you're probably being invited over for dinner and my dad and my mom will be thrilled about this too. So just get ready and I hope you enjoyed your meal."

He smiled. "I did, but I enjoyed the atmosphere most and the company. You've got a great place here. I can see why your customers love it and I'll be anxious to come to your place in Star Gazer Island."

Dora gave her sister a hug. "I'll see you back at the condo. Enjoy your night and no rush. You just keep cooking like you always do. And then I guess we're going fishing in the morning, right?"

Kat chuckled. "Only if you want to. You do not have to get back on that boat. You can spend all your day roaming the town, which I think would be a great idea, or hunting for seashells again. Whatever you want to do, especially this last big day that we're here tomorrow, the full day is your time."

Dora looked at him. "I think it's time to go then. I'll see you tomorrow when you get back tonight or in the morning. See you. Love you."

He rested his hand on the small of her back.

They had paid the bill before all this happened. And then they walked out of the restaurant, out to his Jeep. He helped her in and drove back to the bay.

It took every ounce of willpower in him. Yes, willpower. The want to *not* rush things made him back away. It overpowered, thank goodness, the want to kiss her.

CHAPTER ELEVEN

Dora knew, her sister was going to be full of questions when she got home that night. And since she couldn't sleep, there was no reason to hide out in her room so she waited up for her. The moment Kat walked inside she tossed her purse to the dining table, grinning as if she was overjoyed.

"He is amazing. Not just handsome but unbelievably handsome. Masculine, tall and in comparison to you, my short little sister, *very* tall. And he's your neighbor."

Dora almost laughed at the pure exhilaration in her sister's voice and facial expressions. "So, you're saying that me with a handsome guy is that unbelievable?"

"Not at all. You are a great catch for any man, but

seeing you with this man just has me thrilled. Then that he's from Star Gazer Island and your neighbor, that is completely unbelievably amazing."

Dora agreed. "We both realized that. I was just sitting there eating at the beautiful restaurant watching the ocean when the waitress brought him to the other table right next to me. He was eating alone also and we were both flabbergasted to say the least when we saw each other. But Kat, it really did end up being a wonderful day." She couldn't deny it.

Kat sat down on the couch beside Dora, her beautiful blue eyes, so vibrant. She grabbed her hand. "There is no denying that the two of you were so attracted to each other. I mean, I've never seen that look in your eyes before and it was completely obvious to not just me, but everyone that came around, that that man was so into you there was just no denying it."

Dora couldn't stop the thrill of the words that rambled through her as her sister squeezed her hand. "I just don't know. I mean, he's my neighbor." Now that she was actually talking about it there was a caution that overcame her.

"So, he's nice."

"But, he asked me on a date, a real date, Kat."

Her sister jumped to her feet, her excitement so overwhelming that she couldn't remain seated. "I was right," Kat gushed. "He couldn't resist. This is thrilling, Dora. Me, you know I love my life, but you are so solitary and only making yourself travel because of me, Pearl, and Olivia.

"And today, I feel like I'm going to be able to do a lot of things traveling to my restaurants. But you are a loner so stepping out and dating is a good thing for you."

Dora admitted, "I'm actually excited about it."

"Wonderful. Don't stress yourself out about it, if nothing comes of it, that's okay. You spend a lot of time alone. Too much time."

"I'm starting to think the same thing. Olivia really talked to me about that. She so wanted me to open up and find what she had with our sweet brother. And I'm not saying that this is it. Honestly, I barely know the guy."

"You connected though." Her sister's gaze locked onto hers with encouragement.

"Yes, so I'm going to be brave. He asked me out and I'm going to go."

Kat's expression burst into a vibrant smile. "That's wonderful."

Dora let it all sink in. It felt wonderful and she knew Olivia was smiling too. Hawk was a great man who intrigued her with all his traveling around remodeling houses. But mostly she kept thinking about just sitting with him on her rock and talking to him.

And being held in his arms when she'd stumbled.

* * *

Dora made it home three days after seeing Hawk and she was ready to see him again.

She and Kat had talked again on the long flight home. Kat encouraged her even more this time than during their first talk. Kat was excited that she was looking forward to a date with Hawk.

When they landed then got off the plane, Kat hugged her tight before they got into their cars. Kat was off to another restaurant and Dora was happy for her. She also knew that as much as she had enjoyed her trip, if she hadn't run into Hawk, it wouldn't have been anywhere near as fun as it had been.

He had made it a great trip. Her sister had to, but there was a difference in her sister and the handsome man who made her pulse increase, her heart thunder, and gave her a sense of hope about the next steps involved.

Instead of going to the house she headed to town and to her shop. She would reopen tomorrow and just needed to make sure everything was okay before she turned the open sign and returned to work. She was looking forward to work. She'd spent her last day on Kona walking around town looking at gift shops, checking to see if there was anything she could do to make hers better. She'd thought about driving up and seeing their ranch but didn't. She had a ranch here, so she stayed in town.

But it was instantly evident to her that her store was just as good as the best on the island. That made her happy. She was proud that her love for what she did made her place a great place for tourists. Her little gift store had it all. She smiled as she locked the door, then headed toward her car and saw Lorna McIntyre, the wife of Dallas, had her newest baby with her and was coming down the sidewalk.

"Hey there, it's great to see you," she said, reaching out to wiggle the baby's socked foot, making him chuckle. She loved it.

"He always loves seeing you," Lorna said.

"He's a happy little fella like all your kids. Are you having any more?"

Lorna chuckled. "I might. Dallas said he was good with as many as I wanted to give him."

Dora loved it. This sweet lady had been pregnant when she'd come to town and Dallas had rescued her off the beach where she'd been wandering deep in thought, worrying about her predicament of being alone and an unwed mother when she'd gone into labor. Dallas had been on the way into the back of Star Gazer Inn to see his mother and heard Lorna cry out.

The two of them had been connected from the moment he'd rescued her. Connections came in mysterious and crazy ways sometimes.

"So, how are you doing? I hope you had fun on your trip with your sister. It was odd seeing your store closed but you well deserved the break."

"Thanks, it was a great trip. I'm just not a great traveler, but this trip had a funny turn to it. My new neighbor, I think your husband and his brothers know him, Hawk Harrison. He happened to be there at the same time and we ran into each other."

Lorna smiled huge. "They said he was a great guy and very smart at what he does, redoing and selling property. Was he there doing that?"

"Yes, he was checking on one of his properties before selling it. Odd how small the world can be sometimes."

"Yes it is. Believe me, me and my sweet hubby know how that works. Life has a way of working in its own way. So, are you interested in this new neighbor of yours?"

Dora nodded, she couldn't help it. "I actually am. I know that you had a few fears early on and that's me in some ways. I've never really had a serious relationship. And not sure that's where we're headed, but I am going to go out with him. I just got home and came to check on my store. But I'm heading home now. Not sure where everything goes from there." It hit her then that she'd come to town to avoid going home.

Lorna smiled tenderly as she hugged her baby. "Just relax and get to know him. Enjoy yourself. From what I hear and from what I've seen of you, you basically are a loner and a hard worker, so this might be a good thing. Believe me, I was too. Remember my history."

Dora knew she was a loner and Lorna had gone on a blind date and ended up pregnant, then came to this town and her life had an unexpected great turn. "Thank you for being so open with that. So I'm going to head home and relax. And that little fella is so cute," she said, smiling at the baby, needing the distraction.

"Maybe our little quiet lady in town will one day have one of these cute little babies to hold in her arms." Lorna smiled.

"Maybe." They said goodbye then and she headed to her vehicle and climbed inside while Lorna walked on down the sidewalk. Her words rolled inside Dora's head all the way to her house.

What would it be like to have a child, to fall in love?

It had been on her mind and she couldn't deny that Hawk interested her enough, pulled her enough toward him just by his nearness that that thought hung tight to her heart as she parked her car, unloaded her suitcase, and walked inside her house.

She set her suitcase down in the hallway and then walked straight to the glass windows overlooking the ocean and stared out, feeling peace wash over her. She was home.

And no matter how much everybody thought she needed to travel, this was her peaceful place.

Her gaze went to the rock and she knew she had been hoping to see Hawk sitting on that rock. But he wasn't. However, she knew he'd be calling or maybe this evening he would show up.

CHAPTER TWELVE

Hawk walked to the stone, the rock, hoping she would be there. The moonlight was shining on the water. The waves were soft as they rolled in. It was a very peaceful night. He'd made himself wait and not come out earlier. She had just gotten home today. There was no need to make her feel squeezed, but he hoped and had a feeling that she would be out here. Hoped she'd been serious about going out with him once they got back home.

Home. It had been a long time since he had thought about calling anyplace home, but for some reason, Star Gazer Island felt that way on the ride back from Kona.

That's exactly where his mind had gone.

He had been in his office all afternoon drawing up

plans for the house, remodeling in a unique way, a way that appealed to him, not his usual way of remodeling a house that would appeal to buyers. Something about this home made him want to do it his way.

He spotted her sitting there on the rock, looking out over the moonlight. His heart surrendered. It was a beautiful sight.

The silhouette she made sitting there on that large rock, her knees pulled up, her chin resting on her knees, her arms wrapped around her legs. Peaceful. Happy.

It slammed into him hard that he wanted that in his life. His life was full of constant movement, staying busy. But he was drawn to the rock and to the woman sitting there in the moonlight.

"Hello?" he said quietly, not wanting to startle her.

She turned her head toward him and smiled. "Hello."

"So, how is my neighbor doing?" he asked.

"I'm doing great now that my neighbor is home and I get to see him again," she replied.

"May I?" he gestured to the space beside her.

"Yes, remember half of this rock is yours and I am sitting on my side."

He laughed as he climbed from one small rock to a larger one and then onto the big rock. And then he took a seat, leaving at least two inches between them. Being drawn to move closer so their shoulders touched he forced his strength to hold him back and didn't lean in close. The space was worth it.

He needed to give her time. He needed to give it to himself also because the feelings that he had been feeling ever since he met her and all the way home on the flight were not his usual feelings. He hadn't been able to stop thinking about her. And as he designed the redo of the house, he had her on his mind.

And he started there.

"I've been drawing up plans for my house on the redo and I'm wondering if maybe you'd like to come over and help me look at the drawings. Maybe give me your thoughts of what you, as a lady, would like to see in the remodel."

She smiled. "I would love to do that. I've just always thought that house could be amazing. And as you know, it has almost the same view as my house, which, as far as I'm concerned is the best view in all the world."

He smiled at her, loving the sound of her voice and the fact that she was going to come to his house and help him.

"Great. Then maybe after we figure out when we're going to go have dinner we can go back and you can look at the plans."

"That sounds good," she said.

"So your trip home was good?" Hawk asked.

"Yes, it was," Dora replied. "I just… well I actually didn't buy anything. I wandered around Kona looking at all the gift stores. You know, comparing mine to theirs, seeing if there was anything I could do to make mine better."

"Did you find anything you could do?" he asked.

"No," she said. "I realized it's *my* shop. It has my creative mind inside and my customers come to my shop because everybody that's been there has talked about that. About how real, how loyal my creations are to Star Gazer's special appeal. So, I guess I do it right. I do what makes me happy."

"That's kind of how I do with my remodels. Well, I'm sure you think about this too, but I also think about what will sell, what I like. I'm going to do this new house that I'm in differently." Not sure how she would take it, he continued. "I want it to be a place that I might actually retire at one day. If I ever… I might make it my home base." He almost said *if I ever marry*.

He liked that her eyes flickered in the moonlight at those words as she looked at him. "That sounds like a great plan."

They stared at each other. He wanted so badly to put his arm around her, but he held back.

WHAT'S LOVE GOT TO DO WITH IT

When a breeze blew her hair across her face, he was unable to help himself, he reached up and gently pushed the golden strand behind her ear. His fingers touching her skin sent electrifying radiation through him like nothing he had ever felt—except when they touched.

"You are beautiful," he said, "especially in the moonlight here on your rock." His fingers were still glued to her cheekbone next to her ear where he had pressed the hair gently behind it.

He wanted to kiss her so badly, but he fought off the need, the want. She was special and he didn't want to do anything that would make her push him away. She had told him she wasn't looking for a relationship like he hadn't been, but he felt that maybe, like him, her mind had changed a bit after their Hawaii meeting. He hoped so.

He forced his fingers away and planted them on the rock between their thighs. "When do you want to go eat and where would you like to eat?" he asked, changing the subject from where his mind had gone: *when would you like to kiss or let me kiss you? Or would you even like me to kiss you? Because I want to very badly.* Those were his thoughts.

"Honestly I'm good with anything, it's not like I've actually gone out to eat with a man in a very long time," she said the words quietly.

"I had a feeling you weren't much of a dater. I am not either. But I have my reasons. Do you have reasons why you're not a dater?"

She placed her arms back around her knees and looked out over the water. "Honestly, I just haven't wanted to put myself out there, you know? I'm quiet, I'm a loner. I figured that's the way I was supposed to be..." She paused. "But then you came along and my mind has been rethinking all of that. And my sweet friend Olivia had so wanted me to push myself out there. That was one of her last wishes for me before we lost her. And I had been toying with it."

Her answer pressed hard on his heart. "Olivia must have cared very much for you, for that to be one of her last wishes for you to find happiness. She didn't want you always sitting out here on this rock alone." Unable to stop himself, his hand lifted from the rock and he laid it across her shoulder and gently pulled her in with a light squeeze.

"You are a wonderful person," he said, meaning it with everything inside his heart. "I can see if she'd found love, she was hoping you would find it one day too." That had once been his dream, but it had blown away. But ever since he'd met Dora, his brain had been forgetting all the reasons why he didn't open up to women anymore.

But now, looking at Dora, he knew he wasn't just looking at a female or woman. He was looking at Dora. Sweet, quiet Dora with her big heart. And unable to help himself, he leaned forward and his lips gently met hers, giving her the chance to pull away. But she didn't. His arm drew her closer as kissing her took all of his attention. He knew in that moment that what he felt for this woman was like nothing he had ever felt before.

* * *

She had a date.

The thought had been with Dora all day as she worked in her shop and had more visitors than she had anticipated. Dora was quiet but independent and she loved that people loved her designs. Glad her shop had enough business that money wasn't a problem. She could, if she ever needed to, ask her parents for a loan, but she was able to support herself with her shop and that satisfied her.

Yes, she would inherit more one day but didn't think about that because she wanted her parents around as long as possible. She was independent and had a lovely life. She had a home on the perfect beach and that was enough but she also could fly on the family's private jet to anywhere she needed to go or wanted to go. But to get from her shop to her home she didn't need to fly.

She was blessed and she knew it, but she didn't take advantage of it.

Today she had to talk to herself about it all day long, reminding herself how much she loved her life, because if she didn't think about that her thoughts went instantly to her new neighbor, the amazing cowboy who she had a dinner date with tonight.

It was the first date she had in years, yes, years. Though she had never told anyone, her last date had not been pleasant. And that she thought of often if she'd ever been tempted to accept an offer.

It had been about five years ago, with a man who said he collected intriguing art and creations and he'd heard she carried many great things. He'd seemed nice and they'd talked and even laughed. She'd liked him and felt a connection and accepted his offer to go out to dinner with him. To this day she wasn't sure if he'd just stepped out of line that night or been a man with bad intentions, as her grandmother used to warn her and her sisters about.

"There are scumbags out there," Grandma warned, "Be wary and ready to get away."

Her date with the man she refused to call or think about with any name other than Scumbag, had earned him a knee to his private parts that night. Her sister-in-law Kelley had a similar story but didn't know that when she and Dora talked that Dora had a similar experience. No one in her family knew.

Scumbag had taken her to dinner and then instead of bringing her home, he'd taken her to view the ocean and for a walk on the beach. The moment the car stopped and she went to get out of the car he'd hurried to her side, pulled her into his arms and forced a kiss to her lips… as his hands went places she'd not given her consent for them to go.

Even now her heart thundered in anger thinking about that moment.

Thankfully she reacted with a stomp to his foot, a bite to his lip and her short-legged knee had rammed him in just the right spot. That gave her a moment to race down the beach. For many people she often knew that wasn't enough and the attacker caught up to them. But for her, that night, since she actually knew the beach, it was enough, and she got away. Then again he probably hadn't been able to move for a few minutes after her knee attacked his private part.

She might be small, but she had more strength than anyone might think, especially if she was in panic attack mode. And yes, she did have panic attacks sometimes.

After that night, dating had stopped, and no one in

her family knew that particular part of her life. She'd often worried that she should have told the police about it, so after much thought she'd called and made a report without giving her name. All that led to guilt of keeping silent and worry of it happening again but worse. And so, she hadn't dated. Until now. Nothing about Hawk bothered her, or scared her, nothing.

Everything about the man just drew her. And so, they were going on an actual date. Even when they'd run into each other in Kona she'd felt no fear and she'd even gotten into his Jeep with him. Nothing about that moment had scared her.

And as she drove home that afternoon to get dressed for their date, excitement roared through her. She was finally going on a date with the man that could be the man for her. When she got home she took a swift shower and picked out a nice sundress that had a flowing skirt with colorful sunset tones.

When she had bought the dress, she thought of sunsets on her beach that she loved to watch on the rock alone.

But Hawk had changed that. Hawk had her missing him if he wasn't there. When she heard his truck drive up her driveway, she picked up her small purse and headed to the door just as the doorbell chimed.

She pulled the door open and there he stood.

Stunning in a white shirt, jeans, boots, and he held his straw cowboy hat in his hands at his waist. But it was the smile on his face that drew her. And the thought of his kiss instantly caused her heart to thunder. She had never been kissed like that before.

Never wanted or even thought about a kiss like that before. He totally startled and surprised her last night. His kiss had been tender, no off the wall advance that put alarms into her thoughts. No, Hawk was the man she knew she could think about a future with.

"Hello," he said, smiling.

"Hello to you," she said, feeling off balance suddenly.

"Are you ready to go? You look beautiful," he continued, his gaze sweeping over her and back up to her eyes.

"I'm ready and looking forward to it." Even more than she'd first thought.

He stepped back. "After you," he said, with a sweep of his arm to let her go ahead of him.

She smiled, stepped out the door, pulling it shut as she went. It locked from the inside and she heard the click that assured her it was done. Then she stepped past Hawk, feeling a sense of excitement at his closeness. She headed toward his truck. He was beside her and opened the door, took her elbow as she stepped up onto the step rail, which she needed because she was only five foot four. She settled into the seat and looked at him. "Thanks."

"My pleasure." He lifted his hand and touched her jaw. "I have thought about you all day," he said. Just that simple sentence filled her with a wonderful sensation.

"I thought about you all day too. It's been a very long time since I went on a date."

He looked surprised then nodded. "Me too." Then he closed the door, strode around the front of the truck and slipped into the driver's seat.

Shocked, she looked at him, what had made him not date for a long time?

CHAPTER THIRTEEN

Hawk felt amazed about the shine in Dora's blue eyes, those beautiful blue eyes that had drawn him from day one.

Her golden blonde hair fell over her shoulder as she looked at him. "So where are we going?"

He backed out of her drive, turned onto the gravel road that crossed the ranch to the main road, shifted to drive, all while looking at her. "I thought about it and thought we would go down the road a bit. It's a restaurant I saw and heard was great when I went to Nina McIntyre's art show."

She smiled at him. "That sounds wonderful."

The certainty in her voice shot through him and it was a great feeling. He turned right at the main road and headed toward their destiny. The word destiny echoed through his mind.

They were going to go back to his place after dinner so she could look at his drawings for the house remodel. Thinking about her being comfortable in the house filled him with longing. Having a woman in his life... not any woman, but Dora in his home, in his life.

That was the key.

Dora had opened up things in his heart that he had long pushed away and he knew it from that moment she'd kissed him.

He had never felt that way before, never. "Did you have a good day at work?" he asked.

"Yes," she said instantly as if she too was looking for something to talk about.

They then started talking about their day and the drive went by quickly. Just sitting there listening to her soft voice made his day.

It had him excited about this date, about the anticipation of what could be between them. He just had to be careful, had to not go too fast. He didn't want her to walk away from what he felt building between them.

When they reached the restaurant, it was a small place but had a great deck and view of the ocean. The nice hostess led them to the perfect table.

He thanked her, then she smiled and told him the

waitress would soon be there. He pulled the seat out for Dora then took a seat across from her. It was just a two-seated table, which he liked.

Dora smiled. "I've heard how wonderful this restaurant is, but I've never been here before."

"I heard the same thing so now we'll see. But I'm very happy right now just because you're smiling at me."

Dora chuckled, and so dinner went, great atmosphere and great conversation with the best lady sitting across from him. It was amazing and the food ended up being fantastic. Not that he might really have noticed, because he was so happy to have Dora sitting across the table with him.

When they got back into his truck, they were both smiling.

"So you're sure you want to go look at my place?" Hawk glanced at her as he started the truck.

They had talked about it as they were eating and she really seemed like she wanted to go see. She actually sounded excited about seeing it.

And he was too.

"I do," she said without hesitation and so they went.

The drive went fast, though he didn't speed. And when they drove down a different road than what led to her property because his home was not on their ranch.

He liked how she undid her seatbelt the moment he shifted into park as if really ready to get out and see his designs.

He had pulled into the garage and hurried out but she was already waiting at the door before he was around her side to open the door.

* * *

"I've always loved this house," Dora said, looking excited. "I was here a few times when growing up. Royce, the owner was a sweet man and we would come see him because he was friends with my grandfather. It was always odd that he wouldn't sell the house." She halted her words, startled at what she'd been about to say.

Hawk had unlocked the door but paused before pushing it open. "What brought that sudden look to your face and the halt to your words?"

She gave a cringe then a half laugh. "Before moving Royce decided not to sell the property to our family. I'm embarrassed to say this, and you might have already heard the story, but Royce thought one of us 'little gals' as he called me and my sisters, needed to get married. He didn't sell the property because it is connected to our property and he wanted someone to move in and fulfill his wish and marry one of us."

She laughed, the moment the words came out. Now that she thought about it, it was an odd bit of circumstances that had led her to where she was standing right now.

Hawk smiled, pushed the door open and she stepped inside, needing a little space. "It sounds like he was wishing the best for you and your sisters. As a man from the old days, I'd say he probably didn't really think about how independent women are these days. He probably didn't add your brother in because men are supposed to be independent."

"Exactly," she agreed.

"I haven't met your sister Pearl but you and Kat are very independent and it sounded like y'all aren't really looking. That's what you told me during our first meeting."

"That's right, but anyway, can we see what you're going to do? The place is just like I remember. I think they've done a little bit of updating but nothing major. The kitchen is still as wide open as before and the countertops are the same and the wooden cabinets are older, but it's a large kitchen and with updates can be made amazing."

"You have a vision for property along with your creative sea shell creations."

She smiled. "I guess I do. When I see a seashell, I think of what it could be and how it could become part of a piece of artwork to sell in my store. It's like I like bringing things together."

She realized his smile had widened and her stomach had dipped.

"I get that feeling when I look at a house like this one. I mean, when I walked in, my brain started working and so did yours. Come on, come to my office. You can look at anything you want."

They walked through the kitchen into the large living area that was not as wide open as she would want it to be, but there was a room on the other side that she knew was a little sunroom added on. She had a feeling that this man walking beside her could do anything with this piece of property.

To her surprise, they walked through the living room and into the sunroom, and there was his office.

"I like the sunshine," he said. "I like sitting here in the mornings and evenings, working on things when I come in and looking out over the ocean out there. It's a bit of freedom when I'm busy working. That's why I had thought about using the Kona house as my spot, but I much prefer this spot."

They were standing close, there just inside the door. His arm was brushing hers and sending electrical sensations to her heart. She needed to move so she took a step forward.

"I'm excited to see what your plans are." She walked forward to the large white paper lying on the wide desk. It was the floorplan.

He stepped up beside her. "That's the original floorplan and I'm gearing up to update it. What I don't like to do is jump in instantly and as you know, when I first came here I hadn't really planned on staying. But now I am."

She looked at him, shocked by his words. "You're staying?"

"Yes. I'm going to make this my home spot from here on out."

The thought sent thrills through Dora. Hawk would always be her neighbor. "That's wonderful," she said, breathless.

"I won't stay if you don't want me to."

"No, I think you being here is great."

His expression grew serious as his gaze seemed to dig deep. "If you mean that, maybe we could step forward and think about our relationship? I'm being cautious because I don't want to step over any lines because you're so cautious. I know usually a person has a reason for their cautiousness."

Dora nodded and sat down in one of the two chairs

at the desk, she needed to sit down. Instead of looking at the house plan which was slightly to the side, she looked out through the dark night with the moon glistening on the water. Then she looked at him as he sat down.

She asked the question she needed to know. "What is your story? I mean, why have you never really had a home before?"

He laid his hand on the desk, thumped his forefinger as if thinking. "I had a bad run-in. Well, I call it that sometimes. I fell in love. And then she had an affair and we split up. But several years later she sued me and sued me for abuse." His words shocked Dora but he held her gaze. "I've never touched a woman in an abusive way. Never. I don't talk about this often, but… Dora, I think you need to know everything. I would never ever do anything to hurt a woman."

She reached out and touched his arm. "I get that. I know that. I mean, why would she have done that to you?"

He looked frank. "I have money now. We were younger and I wasn't exactly who I am now as far as finances go. She brought the accusations to get money. But it was all thrown out by the judge. I'm telling you this so you know. I don't want anything coming up later about it."

Dora couldn't imagine anyone saying Hawk was abusive. She'd seen only a gentle but strong man. Yes, some people could be deceptive, she knew this personally but not Hawk. "I don't believe you'd do that."

"I wouldn't, no way. But there are those that lie about it. It was just obvious that she came after me for money so it didn't amount to anything, but I would have fought for my reputation as long as it took. Thankfully now she's remarried and seems happy."

Dora had a feeling the lady probably found another man with money, but she kept that thought to herself. "Thanks for letting me know all of that but I know it's not true. Believe me, I—" She stopped talking. What had she almost said? That she'd lived through almost being raped? "I, I live a simple life and love my life. I could take as much money from my dad and mom as I wanted to, they would give me anything but they love watching us all be independent. I like making my own life. But I can't imagine someone like your ex, even if she wanted your money how could say such awful things about you. I can't see that at all."

He smiled. "Coming from you, that makes me happy. I'm also telling you that so if you need to do some research, I'm fine with that. And your dad is probably already doing that research, or your brother. It makes sense with what your family's worth is that knowing who is around is a good thing. I researched all of you before I bought this property. I know all of you are good people. There's nothing about me that you need to worry about. I wanted to be honest with you up front now that we have a chance of maybe moving forward, so that when you learn the history, you will not think wrong of me. To me, that is the most important thing."

He hesitated then continued. "Dora, I've never said this to anyone before. I want you to know me for the man I am, the man I have worked hard to be, and mostly for the man I want to be and that is the man in your life."

I want to be and that is the man in your life. Hawk's words roared through her.

"Dora, take a breath," Hawk said gently.

"Friends, we are neighbors," she said.

"We are... and interested?" he asked with a smile.

Now he smiled at the beginning. "A new beginning between you and me. Friends, neighbors, and I'd like a new start."

"So tell me now, what do you think you want to do here? I mean, I see this area that you've taken in as your office as a bigger area of the living room that could be spectacular, widened and enlarged." She paused.

He grinned. "Do you see a window up above that

maybe I can get your sister-in-law to design? I have it on my mind and it won't go away. This wall that we're looking at right here would be joined in with the larger living room like you're imagining but have a glass window up above also and wide glass doors that slide back if you want them to. A huge patio. I just have it in my mind. What do you think about that?"

"I love it. See, I live in a small place but I love it because I have the glass doors I can walk through the back door and immediately see out at the ocean and it draws me in. So imagine even if you didn't feel like going outside and sitting there on the porch, you could still look up at the sky."

Her voice grew softer. "Again, I have Olivia on my mind. In the end she could sit on the couch and, well, me and my brother had talked about how much she would have loved to have one of Kelley's windows in the ceiling."

"I think it's a great idea."

They stared at each other.

"Then that's what we're going to get done, because we all agree. I just have to see your sister-in-law and see what schedule she has. And I'm a builder. I'd love it if she can design it for me and tell me who to get to install it. I'm all good."

Dora smiled. "Well, you're in luck, I think, because

tomorrow is Saturday. We could go and see her 'cause she's home from her traveling. And... if you need a man that's really good at redesigning and doing things, the owner of Star Gazer Island, her husband, he is a great guy at redoing. And I bet that he could help. Of course I don't know his deadlines or anything like that. That would have to be checked on."

"I think me bringing you over here to talk about this was a great idea because yes, tomorrow is Saturday. Aren't you working?"

"I hired someone to help me out and she comes in on Saturdays. That way I can take some time off if I want. And tomorrow I want to."

"Then it's a deal. You tell me what time and I'll be there." He smiled. "Now I guess I need to carry you home."

"How about first we take a walk on the beach? I'd love to walk on your beach. We could go on the rock and then I could go to my home that way."

"Are those sandals you're wearing okay to do that in?"

"Yes, because I'll take them off. I can climb that rock at any time of day and I really think sitting on the rock right now would be a wonderful thing to do."

"That's two of us. Come on, my neighbor lady, let's do this."

WHAT'S LOVE GOT TO DO WITH IT

He stood up, held his hand out. She placed hers in his and felt the sizzle of the man race through her.

They walked outside the back door. The light was fading and the moonlight was beautiful as they walked down the walkway that led to the small gate that opened up to his beach. Her beach separated by a rock. They walked down the beach to their rock and then together, him helping her. Just being careful. She knew she didn't need to say, "I can do this," instead she let him help her because once again she didn't want to stumble and they'd both end up hurt. She didn't want to do that again because this time they might not be so lucky and she might hit something and not be able to enjoy their wonderful evening that they were having.

When they reached the top of the rock, he held her arm as she sat down and then he sat down beside her. Their arms touched. They both pulled their legs up and their knees touched, her leg and his leg.

She loved it.

And the moon… goodness the moon was amazing. Just like the man.

CHAPTER FOURTEEN

Hawk had lain awake last night after having sat at the table, looking at the drawing. He knew he could tear the wall out, open up the closed space of the house like his heart was opening up, rebuilding from the inside out. This house was the most important house he'd ever remodeled. This house would be rebuilt in the hope that Dora, the woman he loved, would love him too.

He had never before felt what he felt for Dora. Every ounce of his being wanted to be near her. To see the smile on her face. Wanted to hold her close and experience love. Real love.

Yet he knew he couldn't rush her. She might not feel the same way. They had just known each other for a short time, but for him it had been the best days of his life and as he closed his eyes so sleep would happen and he would see her again tomorrow, he knew nothing would ever compare to the way he felt about Dora.

Morning came quick and then finally he picked Dora up the next day a little before noon and drove down to the amazing house just down the road. They were having lunch with Matt and Kelley on the patio. He would finally get to meet the amazing builder he'd researched and the man his heart hurt for. But was happy Matt had known true love and found it a second time with Kelley. It was something. Hawk was now hoping he could have one great love story. He'd had a terrible ending on his first marriage, but obviously the love Matt had shared with his first wife had lived beyond death, and that was not what Hawk had experienced. That was true love.

First, they passed her father's house, which was a big ranch house that overlooked the bay and he could tell as they passed that it had a large patio on the back of it also. So further down the coast and pastures of cattle they came to the house that had an amazing view. He could not wait to see the view from the back of the house through the windows and the roof.

And as Dora had said, the glass doors. "You're excited, aren't you," she asked.

"I am. I find it to be unique having researched everything she creates and hearing the reviews and the lady has a busy life, I think."

"Yes, she does. My brother does too, running the ranch. It's huge as you can tell, and oil too. They have meetings everywhere and sometimes they can travel together. But they have found when he's traveling they have a life in between and both are preparing well it' easier for him to prepare for babies than for her because she is the one who travels so much. But she said she would slow down when the time is right. And like you're wanting her to do, she doesn't always build the entire house, just works with unique builders, great builders, to get it done right."

"That's what I found in my research. I saw that Kelley and her crew came in and installed her sky windows and that's what gave me the idea."

"I should have known you researched that. You think of everything and research it all."

He reached across the truck and gently touched her arm. "I do, that's why I knew you'd be a great neighbor."

"Good to know. And my brother is too."

"I figure he looks out for his sisters."

"Yes he does."

They went in the house and the door was drawn

open by her brother. They introduced themselves and Matt studied him with serious eyes then looked to Dora. "Hey, Seashell." Matt gave Dora a hug.

Hawk zeroed in on the perfect nickname for Dora and the protective way Matt was hugging her. It was a message that Hawk got the instant his gaze met Matt's as he hugged his sister. Matt was telling his sister he had her back with that hug while at the same time telling Hawk he was watching.

It was exactly what a brother should do and Hawk nodded at him in acknowledgment as Matt released Dora. Hawk liked knowing Dora had someone watching over her.

He also got the feeling as they walked through the amazing house that they had agreed to this meeting so quickly because Matt wanted to check him out. He liked that too.

When they reached the living room it was amazing. The large glass wall of sliding doors to the outside gave an open room experience to the outside, and the huge glass window in the ceiling with the sunlight shinning through opened it up even more. The sun sent colorful spots of sparkles twinkling around the room as it reacted to the beautiful jeweled ornament hanging from the ceiling rod, It had been made by the renowned ornament maker, Myla Hudson who lived in Mule Hollow . This ornament like many of hers was made with real jewels and sold at auctions for huge amounts. But like Dora, she also made affordable ornaments for everyone else. Similar to Dora's seashell shop.

"Hi," said the pretty lady he assumed was Kelley. "I waited for you to come inside so I could see your reaction when you walked into my living room." She smiled big. "You get it."

"Yes, I get it. It is amazing. Wow." The room was outstanding. "It's one thing to hear about your creations, but to see it, it is phenomenal."

"Thank you. I love it too. It takes my world to new heights and others too."

"That's what everyone says and I see it. The beautiful jeweled ornament is outstanding too." Hawk looked from the amazing window creator to her husband who was also looking up at the ornament shining in the light.

"It encompasses my life," Matt said. "My life with my first love and the beginning of my life with my new love." He looked straight at Hawk. "You, neighbor, have chosen the right woman to do an amazing creation for you."

Hawk liked the way Matt thought. He was strong and knew something outstanding when he saw it. This ornament and his wife were obviously cherished as was his previous life and wife.

He looked at Dora and saw in her expression that she too got where her brother was coming from in his thoughts.

She smiled at Hawk and he was instantly thankful he'd moved in next door to Dora.

* * *

"Welcome to my world," Kelley said, drawing him back to reality to look at her big smile. "I'm so excited that you want to take our house next door and put one of my designs in. I call them sky ceilings because it's bigger than a skylight, you know? And I researched you. You do a lot of homes all over the place. That's interesting."

He smiled, glad to meet this remarkable woman. "I have researched you also and you have a wonderful story and an incredible ability. I'm so glad you were able, with the help of Matt, to get back to your world. And I have to say this is mind-boggling. I love it and I'd love for you to come and look and plan for the house next door to Dora's land because my thoughts on it are going to be wide open. No limits.

"I see by the look on everyone's faces as you scan the room. Yes, I am a wanderer. I've not put my roots down in a long time but I knew when Jackson and Nina had the art show and when I bought her painting, I had a feeling that I would love the house and I came directly here and yeah, I loved it, and my brain is working overtime on what I want to do with it."

Matt waved to a chair. "Do you want to sit or do you want to go outside on the patio? We're going to have lunch out there, but I'm interested in knowing what your plans are. I mean, it is a great place and well, to be honest, we wanted to buy it, but Mr. Johnson didn't want to sell it to us."

"And that's his right."

"We don't hold that against him either. Everybody has that right. So no hard feelings on that. We're glad you're there. And are you thinking of staying there, or are you traveling?"

"I love it inside here, but let's go out on the patio. I want to see the outside also and I am going to stay for a while. I think this is going to be my home office. My starting point, ending point."

Once he saw it, he knew. He didn't say that once he saw Dora, he knew. He didn't add that, he didn't think that would be a smart move on his part. But he saw Matt tilt his head and he knew Matt was thinking the same thing. At least Matt didn't look wary. He looked interested like a brother should be. If he had a little sister, as small as Dora especially, that'd be him. He'd be looking out for her.

"And as you all know, I have great neighbors, especially this little lady right here."

Kelley walked over to the table that was set, patted the seat beside where she pulled her seat out. "This is for you, Dora. You can sit by me and the two guys can sit over there and let's enjoy this meal that I didn't make. Y'all know I don't cook that much, but we had it delivered from Star Gazer Inn, and I know it's going to be wonderful."

Matt grinned. "I cook, but I came in from over at the office and I let my lovely wife take care of business."

Kelley chuckled. "Yes, he's learned that when I'm taking care of business, everybody better get out of my way because I'm going to do it." That got smiles from everyone including Matt. "I'm going to do it my way."

She pulled the top off her plate and motioned for everybody else to do the same and it was a delicious-looking club sandwich. She smiled. "Not sure what everybody likes, so I figured a club sandwich, they make amazing ones, and those great potatoes on the side would do fine. If you don't like one of the meats just take it off."

He liked her. She had a mind of her own.

Dora grinned. "Yes, I think I know what you're thinking. Yes, she has a mind of her own. I think it's even more amazing when we first met her; our poor sister-in-law couldn't step inside a building because of the fear that filled her. Determination and Kelley go hand in hand."

Kelley reached out and gave her sister-in-law a quick hug around the corner of the table. "Yes it does," she said, looking at him. "Life is a mystery sometimes. I've gotten through with God's help and Matt's help and all this family. But in the beginning, sweet Matt there… determination and a work-hard spirit can carry you through just about anything. And thank the good Lord my overworking creative mind didn't give up on me.

"Sometimes I say, well you know that song that Shania Twain made famous, 'Love Is Everything.' Well, I'm getting sidetracked, but… I do know that from what I understand she was going through a lot when she sang that song and I have a feeling…" She paused. "But I can tell you in my life, love has everything to do with it."

She smiled at her husband and reached out and put her hand in his open hand, waiting for hers.

Hawk watched them as the song rang in his thoughts. He knew without a doubt he wanted that. Those two had been through a lot to find love, happiness in life. He forced a smile. "I like it. I think your story is amazing. Would make a fantastic movie."

Dora nodded. "I think so too. It's an amazing story, especially if you add in how they met, my brother going to find his dog, Healer who is out roaming and found her with a rattlesnake behind the house. She was just coming out of the shower with the pistol. My brother is a good shot but I can tell you one thing. My sister-in-law, she is an amazing woman with a gun. That rattlesnake didn't stand a chance."

He laughed. "What a story," he said. "It definitely would make a movie."

Kelley smiled. "That's just part of what makes this marriage work. And that's what I put into everything I do, just so you know. We're going to go over and look at your house whenever you want us to. After we eat if you want, because I'm excited about it. If you don't have someone to help with your remodel, I can find you someone. But my men put my glass in, whether I'm involved in the whole project or not."

"That's what I found out in my research. And that's perfect. I have crews too. But can hire local for this."

"Dora, what do you think about his house?"

"It's a great place and we went there last night and it needs updates but Hawk has a good eye and his ideas and the plan is evolving. I get exactly where he's going to put the sky ceiling."

Hawk saw out of the corner of his eye Matt and

Kelley exchange sweet glances, and he had a feeling that they both probably knew he had his eyes on Dora. Thank goodness, at that moment a black and white dog, an Australian Shepard, came barreling around the corner of the house.

"Healer," Dora exclaimed, sliding from her chair to her knees as the dog bounded up to her and instantly placed both his front feet on her shoulders and they hugged. She looked at him over Healer's shoulder. "This is the special dog in our family's life."

Healer placed his paws on the ground and spun to Hawk. The dog had a protective instinct it was clear. Hawk held his hand out and thankfully he passed inspection as the dog moved so Hawk could rub his head.

Everyone at the table smiled.

"You've passed inspection," Dora said.

"Great. I'm relieved," he said, and smiled back at the lady smiling at him.

CHAPTER FIFTEEN

"She likes that cowboy," Matt said to his smiling wife the minute they got into their truck after the tour of Matt's house.

"Yes, she does. She's not really excited about showing us that, but she did without knowing it, I think. Dora is so amazing. Outgoing when you get to know her, quiet if you don't. She's just a combination of both. From the first moment I met her when they all came to help you with what you were going through after Olivia…"

He grinned at his wife. "Poor you. You owe her what?" he asked, knowing what she was going to say or at least thinking he did.

"I hope to offer her help if I can give it to her like

she gave to you and me. I mean, you know your sisters, they dream of, well, they're all so into their business and traveling. And I get it. I was there too, but I have found out that I can do both. I can have the love of my life and the life with me and still build these wonderful inspirations that God gives me in my head. And I want them to feel that too, but I can't just bring it out."

"So, like with Dora, I believe if this is the right guy, and for some reason I feel like it is, then we need to help out if we can. But I have a feeling that Hawk is being cautious because he knows it too."

They were driving down the road now, heading to the house, and Matt's thoughts were deep on his sister.

"None of us talk about it much. But Dora hasn't always been so quiet. You know, she did date early on, and suddenly, no, she didn't. So, my sisters and I stayed out of it. I had my own stuff going on. I mean, I was busy on the ranch and, you know, she's my sister, but Pearl and Kat, they let me know that they knew something, too, maybe that they just had a little bit of time to talk to her and they gave her moments to open up, but she has never said what it was. And that's her. That's her privacy. I can't as a brother cross that. So I am thrilled to see that she actually has her eyes on someone. And we agree, he seems like a great guy."

"Yes. I'm not sure where your sisters are at the

moment. Maybe we can all talk, have a… you know, all of them at the same time, have a FaceTime with each other or something."

"Yeah. We might do that. I'll check into it. But right now, I'm gonna take you home. I know you're going to be going and packing and heading out tomorrow. So I want us to enjoy the day. And I know your brain is already working on what to do. You gave him Nate's number, and he knows who likes his work. So that'll be a great thing. And it'll all get planned out."

"So anyway. As a brother, I'm trying not to be invasive or a matchmaker. I know for me, I had my moments, you know, with my sister, we don't want to overstep."

"No, we don't, I understand, so, that'll be entirely up to you."

She smiled. "The last thing I want to do is upset Dora. I love the way her blue eyes sparkle, but then she had this deep look on her face. It makes me think maybe she was thinking about something serious. Maybe you're right, we need to stay out of it for a little while."

"Yes, I think you're right."

He reached over and placed his hand over hers, squeezed gently. "I am so thankful you are in my life. I love you very much."

Kelley McIntyre's smile went through and through

him. He had been blessed twice in his life. Twice. It was amazing. He'd loved Olivia with all his heart and never thought he'd be able to do what she'd wanted him to do, begin again. And then he'd met Kelley and lost his heart again. He wanted his sisters to know how it felt to be loved like that. But he couldn't step over the line. He could just protect them as much as possible.

* * *

Dora loved the idea of helping Hawk redo this amazing house.

They spent the afternoon, the entire Saturday afternoon, sitting out on the porch, him with his pen and paper talking about what would be great, what she thought would be the best thing, and he had been point blank telling her, "Pretend it's your house, just pretend. I mean, what would you as the lady of the house want here? Because I don't have a lady of the house, but if I ever do, I want it to appeal to her."

Dora had listened to his words carefully. And in her heart of hearts she wished it was her, because she wasn't going to assume anything, wasn't going to step across that line, and yet he was being cautious too. She couldn't figure out if it was because he was afraid to worry her or if he cared for her as much as she got the idea he did when he looked at her.

Whatever it was, she liked the man, liked him with all of her heart.

She had never said she loved any man other than her father and her brother. She loved them with a daughter's heart and a sister's heart. But never had she loved a man with a woman's heart. A heart of love.

She guessed she was chicken because she couldn't step across that line. Even though she wanted him to kiss her again. She wanted to feel what she'd felt being in his arms. Feeling secure, feeling wanted, needed, loved. That's how she'd felt.

So she sat, pushing her crazy thoughts away as she stared at the words on the paper where he had written thoughts on the kitchen.

"The kitchen could use an update," Hawk said.

"Yes, it could. I mean, I can tell when it was built it was built well, but I agree with you. It definitely needs an update."

"So, what are your thoughts on that? White? I mean, do you think it deserves white? Tile, and of course the countertop, most important thing of all, and the bar area is going to have a gigantic island."

"Not a bar, an island," she said. "I've been in a lot of houses and I love the ones that were open to the living area with a gigantic bar, I call it a bar, but I mean an island where food can be prepared. And I'd like one day to be able to do that for me and my family.

"You're planning on having a family one day?" She couldn't help but ask.

He smiled at her. "I am. I hadn't really thought about it for a long time. But now I know I do. I want a family. I want to raise it here. I want to live like you and your sisters and brother have on this beautiful coastline and this wonderful town of Star Gazer, and the surrounding areas. I feel at home here."

She smiled all the way to her heart and knew she wanted to be the woman in this house with this amazing man. Hawk was his name, and like a hawk, she zeroed in on him in that moment.

"I think that whatever woman you fall in love with will feel blessed and will love this house where you can raise a family together," she said. They shared a look with each other. She felt as if they were both at a line drawn in the sand. She just couldn't step over the line, and he didn't seem like he was ready to step over the line either.

Then she stood up. "I like white. I like white cabinets that open it all up. You've got so much woodwork and you've got more woodwork. So I like white and the countertops. I'm sure they'll be beautiful when you go to pick them out."

"Well, that'll be a little ways down the line, but maybe if you still like me, whenever we do that, you can go help me pick them out."

She laughed. "So that's the problem. You're thinking I might not like you by the time you get through with this remodel."

He laughed. "Oh, you've not been through remodels like me. They can have hard moments. I can't imagine being through one with another person making the decisions. But I'm enjoying making them with you."

She smiled. "Great, then we're going to do this."

So they worked on ideas for the kitchen. His mind overflowed with information on housing and remodeling and all kinds of things, and she just listened to him rattle on in a wonderful way. She loved it actually, and then she realized it was almost dinner time.

"Oh my goodness, I need to go," she said.

He stood up. "I'll give you a ride."

She smiled real big. "It's okay." She looked at her shoes. "I can slip these off and walk around the rock."

He smiled at that. And then before she took a step, he stepped toward her and embraced her. Her heart stopped at the feel of his arms going around her.

* * *

Hawk had tried to keep his mind off the woman helping

him so enthusiastically to get the remodeling of the house started. She seemed much better than earlier when he had seen that look on her face that had disturbed him.

It was getting late now, but he still wondered what it was that troubled her. But now, not able to help himself, she was going home and he was holding her in his arms, exactly where he wanted her.

"Dora," he said softly. "Thank you for everything. I'm very glad I moved in next door to you, that I met you, and that I'm getting to know you. And that you're letting me hold you in my arms."

She looked up at him, those blue eyes of hers touching his heart. "It's been a great day," she said softly.

She hadn't pulled away and so he lowered his lips to hers. Instantly she reacted by kissing him back as her arms wrapped his waist, hugging him like he needed, wanted her too. And he was where he wanted to be for the rest of his life. Right here in the moonlight with Dora in his arms.

He didn't care if he traveled anymore. He didn't care if he remodeled houses anymore. He just wanted to have this woman in his life. He deepened the kiss and embraced her stronger and she responded by holding on to him tighter.

He pulled away, knowing he had to talk instead of

kiss. "Dora, I don't want to scare you away. But I have *very* deep feelings for you."

She reached up with her hand and touched his lips with her finger. "I have feelings for you too, like I've never felt before."

His heart lunged. "Same for me. I'm so glad I moved in here."

Her lips lifted. "I'm so glad you moved in next door to me too." Then she pulled back slightly. "But I need to go now. We… we'll get all our thoughts in order along the way as we remodel your house." Then she backed out of his arms and walked quickly out the door.

He followed her, but not closely, as she needed space. Why had he thought that from the beginning? Yes, he'd thought it but now he knew it.

In the moonlight she disappeared onto the beach and he strode out to the edge watching her through the moonlight as she walked to her rock then up and over it instead of around it since the water was up.

He strode quickly to the rock and to the top just to make sure she got home okay. She was almost to her yard, and she turned. "I'm safe. Thanks for following me and making sure."

He hadn't tried to hide it. "I didn't want to pressure you but I'm glad you're home safe. Sleep good, Dora."

And then he turned and headed back down the rock.

This was a turning point. She hadn't said no. She hadn't closed him off. So in the next days, or months, if that's what it took for sweet Dora to open up to him, he would be here.

CHAPTER SIXTEEN

Over the next few weeks, Dora had more fun than she'd had maybe in her entire life.

She worked at her store, creating things as her two new ladies came in and took care of the store and sales. If she wasn't at the store or on the beach collecting sea shells she went around the rock and met Hawk.

Seth Roark, Alice's husband, was now the main construction man on the job. He had helped his wife build an amazing area behind the Star Gazer Inn and remodel the inside too. As far as Dora was concerned, there was no one better for this job. Like Hawk, who had the eye of a hawk when zooming in on buys, Seth had the ability to make it happen. Despite the near twenty years in age difference, he and Hawk got on great.

This man she was crazy about had great taste. And he knew how to choose the right people through the advice of others and his own judgment. But unlike some people, he didn't think his was always the right advice, so he sought, thought about it, and made the move on whichever one he decided was the best. But he always took things into consideration. Like everything she suggested, he went with but there were times that he added something to it to make her suggestion better. And that made her happy. The man made her better too and she knew it. And the way he looked at her, smiled at her, and talked with her about life and work, she felt like he loved having her around.

That crazy woman who'd accused him of abuse had wanted his money and there was no getting around that. This man was a good man.

A man who loved her opinion on all things. He would say, "Hey, Dora, come put your thoughts in on this." He would smile and she would go over near him, where she loved to be and together, they would make decisions. They were a great team.

They had known each other all of six weeks now. And after that first kiss on the beach when he told her he cared for her, and she had put a halt to his words in a soft way that he had listened to. No pressure from him but there were kisses under the sun sometimes, and under the moon. But he never tried crossing the line she'd drawn.

He'd never let his kiss go too long, and she knew it was because for some reason the man knew something deep inside of her was bothering her.

Today had been another great day and though she didn't want to talk about her past lately, her thoughts had been driving her crazy. During all the happiness she was experiencing, she was still feeling that heavy heart.

"I like doing this with you," he said as he walked her to their rock.

She looked up at him, her heart full. "I like it too. You're going where tomorrow?" she asked, knowing he had a trip.

He smiled. "I'm flying out to a home I bought on the San Juan Islands just outside Friday Harbor. It's a beautiful place. Have you ever been to that island or any of the islands?"

"No, I haven't. You buy houses in the oddest places. It's just all over the place, it seems."

"I have this thing inside me that likes to see the world. And when I'm there, I look at real estate. And I'm very blessed to be able to buy it if I want it, if I see a potential to make money off of it. And I saw a great potential on the one in San Juan. It's a great island. And where the house sits, you can actually see the orcas when they come through."

"Really. That's wonderful. And a selling point, I'd think."

"It is. Would you want to go? I mean, you'd have your own room. I'd take you out to eat one night. We'd see the orcas if they're there. I think it's this time of year."

She should say no. "Actually, I think that would be wonderful."

"You trust me, right?"

She smiled. "Yes, I do trust you. I trust you very much."

"Then meet me here in the morning at seven."

"I'll do that." She stood on her tiptoes and kissed him with a quick brush of her lips. She made that move, not him, and she couldn't help it. This was like a step in a new direction and she liked it.

And most important of all—she trusted him.

* * *

The next morning Dora drove her vehicle to his house. She was excited, thinking about the trip and her trust in him was so important for her.

She had just gotten inside her house last night when her phone rang. She looked at it. It was a conference call from her sisters on FaceTime. She could see them and they could see her. She clicked the switch.

"Well, hello, traveling sisters. How are y'all?" she'd asked, suddenly feeling like she was crossing a line and would be a traveling sister also. Two trips within a six-month period was huge for her.

Her sisters were both grinning at her. "We are great. Well, I'm great," said Kat.

"I'm wonderful," added Pearl. "I've heard so many great things from Matt, Mom, Dad, and Kat. They actually said that you're helping remodel the house with Hawk. I *love* that name, Hawk. Is he as strong as an eagle? Is he steady? Strong?" Pearl hitched her brows.

Dora laughed.

Kat laughed too. "Or, since he seems to fly like an eagle and see from far away a house he can make huge dollars from, I'm thinking his name should be Eagle rather than Hawk."

Dora had sat down in her chair. "Actually, y'all, he does all of that. Hawk is his nickname, Harper is his real name. And you're right, Kat, the man does have the eye of an eagle. He sees something and knows what it *could* be, not what it is. And that's why he bought the place next to me. It's looking amazing. And he got Seth, Alice's husband, to help him with the design and our sweet sister-in-law to design a ceiling and her crew came over and is getting the roof ready. By the time we get home next week, they'll be ready to put in a glass ceiling."

As she was talking, she noticed both sisters went on alert.

"Where are you going?" Pearl asked.

"Are you going on a trip?" Kat asked. "Our sister who never goes anywhere unless we beg her to?"

She laughed. It was so true. "Actually, I am. I'm flying with Hawk to a house he's about to remodel and it's on the San Juan Island."

"And you said yes?" Kat asked, astonishment on her expression.

"I did. He asked if I might want to go and look at it and have dinner and I said yes. I'll have my own room," she made sure to clarify. "And I trust him, so I'm excited. I've got to pack and we're flying out of here in the morning in his helicopter to where we'll get on the plane and then we'll be there."

Her sisters, for the first time in her life, were quiet. Just staring at her. "Okay, y'all can talk now, and if you're worried about anything, don't be. Believe me, I know who to trust and who not to trust even though y'all think I'm so quiet."

Both sisters smiled hugely. "Oh, we trust you," Kat said. "We've just been waiting for *you* to trust yourself.

I think this is wonderful. What an adventure!"

"Matt said you and Hawk got along wonderfully," Pearl said, "and that you were helping with the house, and the house was looking great. And you know, we all look out for each other."

"Exactly," Kat agreed. "We just actually called to talk because we haven't all three talked in forever."

"I've missed y'all," Dora said, loving their connection. "I haven't seen you in at least six weeks, Pearl."

Pearl smiled. "I've been working on these jobs, one turned into several, but I'm almost finished. I came over here to Switzerland and I started working on artwork photos for one company, and then another company called and now I started working for them and have another offer too. It's been a lot. I've loved it. I've traveled all over Switzerland taking photos of beautiful places and then having them mounted in several beautiful hotels over here. It's breathtaking. I love it."

Dora loved how adventurous her sisters were and that they saw the world, and she was thrilled that she was about to see a part of the world that she had never seen. And she was going to see it with Hawk. "Both of you love seeing the world. And I'm excited to see a little more of it myself."

Both of her sisters' eyes widened. She loved her

sisters and loved that they cared enough for her to be worried and to call her just to check on her. "So other than checking on me, is there anything else going on that I need to know?" she asked them, but they both smiled and said no.

"It was just time for us to talk. Sisters. Three sisters," Pearl said, with that amazing smile that she had. Not a grin, it was just beautiful. She looked like a pearl with her soft-toned skin and near-white blonde hair.

"I love y'all," Dora had said.

And they both had said the same thing.

And then she stood up. "Okay, I hate to cut it short, but we're leaving early and I've got to pack. We're only going to be there for two nights so we'll get there and look around. We'll have that evening for dinner and then we'll spend the day finishing up his business and going around the island, and he said maybe getting a boat and going out and see the orcas if they're there. I want to see the whales. I've always heard beautiful things about them. It would be awesome. And then we come home the next day so he and I can both be back to work. And when we get back, Kelley's team will be putting in the ceiling window. The sliding doors are already in. It's amazing. It's going to be similar in many ways to our brother's house, but different. The atmosphere is different. I love it. I love their house too, but this, I helped create."

That was true. They said goodbye and she hurried and packed. Now, it was morning already and here she was driving up to the house with the helicopter waiting.

He was standing near the house that she'd almost told her sisters was their house, hers and Hawk's. She couldn't go that far. But as she saw him standing there, she knew with all her heart she wanted to.

The helicopter that she hadn't even noticed before sat back behind the big red barn on a concrete pad that was made for it. He had said he did it that way so people didn't just drive by and notice he had a helicopter sitting there, and it was smart. He'd said he didn't like it being out there in front of everybody.

He was smiling when she drove up. "Pull in the garage," he said, waving her to the first open door. His truck was in the second spot. "This will protect it and keep it out of view."

She knew he didn't want rumors to spread if anyone saw her SUV parked at his home for days. She was thankful for his thoughts. However, she'd been thinking about living in his house with him… as his wife. Something that had kept her from sleeping last night.

He opened her door and smiled. "It's a great day for flying. Good morning, traveling buddy."

She grinned, feeling so happy at the smile and light

gleaming from his eyes. "I'm excited."

"Even better then." He opened the back of her SUV and pulled out her bag. "Is this it?"

"That's it."

He took the bag, closed the door and then after putting the garage doors down they walked to the helicopter. Then he took her hand as she stepped up and settled into the seat.

"There you go. I got to thinking that I didn't ask if you get nervous on planes or helicopters?" He was still standing next to her on the outside of the helicopter.

She took a breath. "I do get a little bit nervous on a plane, but I've honestly never ridden in a helicopter. And I did better on my last trip on the plane, so I'm determined to do good here. I can do this."

"Yes, you can," he smiled, then reached across her, grabbing the seatbelt and calmly buckled her in, checking it to make certain with a little pull that it was secure. Then, he backed up and closed the door.

Her heart was thundering not from the ride she was about to have but because of the man whose nearness was now undeniable to her heart.

He climbed in from the other side and handed her headphones. "Put these on," he said as he placed his on, then said hello. She heard him loud and clear.

Within seconds, the helicopter blades were

churning and the small helicopter lifted off the ground and into the air. Dora's insides rumbled, but she focused on the beauty and the fun of lifting straight up then, the front dipped and they headed toward the ocean. And she loved it.

"This is different from a plane. I can see why you like this helicopter," she said, watching below, seeing her beach, her rock, correction, their rock, and her small house. She looked back and saw his house. It was beautiful. Across the water they flew and she saw her parents' house, her brother's house, and then as they flew along the coast, she spotted the Glamping camp from the air. "This is an awesome way to get to the airport."

He grinned. "I'm addicted to it. I've been flying for a long time, so have no worries. I'm not a crazy flyer, and I'll get you there safely."

And he did. They landed at the small airport, a private airport, and then within minutes, they were approaching a private jet.

"So you have a jet too?" she asked, startled by the elegant jet waiting for them.

"No. I use Beck McCoy, who owns McCoy Jets Company. I'm one of their frequent flyers. Have you heard of them?"

"Yes, Dad uses them sometimes for us whenever

his plane is busy. Well, for my sisters. Like I said, I don't fly that much, only when I have to." But Beck McCoy was one of the McCoy billionaires who were well know all around. They also had a huge ranch in the Texas Hill Country and came to the McIntyre cattle auctions.

They had reached the jet. "How are you feeling?"

She smiled. "Honestly, I'm enjoying myself. I feel a little more adventurous than I've felt in a long time."

They were almost to the sleek jet and to her surprise she saw it was none other than the handsome owner, Beck, standing by the short stairs. She smiled. "Hi, Beck."

"Hello, I heard you were coming on this trip and I decided to be your pilot today. I am glad to see you."

"I didn't even ask who the pilots were. He was just telling me that he uses your company and I think that's awesome. The world is small sometimes, isn't it?"

"Yes, it is," Beck said. "Will all of you as a family be at the McIntyre horse and cattle sale next week? We'll all be there."

"I'll be there. Dad has already made sure I'm going to help buy heifers for him."

"You do have an eye for it. Are you bringing Hawk with you? I hear he's looking for cattle since he's settling down."

Startled by Beck's words, she looked at Hawk, who was smiling. "I'm not sure. Are you going?" she asked.

"I've been invited and I'm planning on going. I need some cattle and I've heard from others like Beck that you have a great eye for picking the heifers that can carry calves well."

She hitched a shoulder. "It's an important pick for a cattleman. Mama cows carrying a calf and feeding it is one of the most important parts of the business. And well, I'm good at it."

He grinned. Actually, grinned, and so did Beck. "That's great. I like it. So will you help me buy the cattle that will start my cattle ranch out right?"

Beck's grin turned big. "I can tell you, this short gal might be quiet, but she's knows cattle. She knows horses too."

"Horses too. So you are a cowgirl."

Dora laughed, couldn't help it. "I'm a sea shell hunter and a cattle-loving cowgirl who enjoys seeing if I can choose the best. Dad and Matt always ask me to help them choose both. Of course they're good at it. They just want to include me."

"Don't believe her," Beck said. "You'll see what I'm talking about when she starts walking through the stalls with her alert eyes zeroed in."

"This I have to see." Hawk was intrigued more than

ever now by Dora.

"Yes, I'll help you. I used to help buy all the time, then my heart went to what I do with sea shells. So I don't help on the ranch anymore. But I can ride and I have an eye for great choices in animals, and they trust me."

"I trust you too. How about helping me that night? I can pick you up if you go with me, but if you don't want to go with me, you could still help me out."

Beck gave her a nod. "I'll go get the plane ready. You know how to board?" He turned then, a grin on his face as he gave them space. She'd always like the cowboy airplane-flying man and liked him more now. He knew his business, and giving people who rode on his private planes their privacy was part of the glamour and reason he did so well.

"Sure, I'd help you," she said to the man standing by her side. "I think that's great actually. And yes, you can pick me up."

"Awesome. Now watch your step, young lady, as you climb up into this small jet."

They climbed on board, and within moments the doors were closed. Their seats were beside each other, and Beck and his co-pilot waved at them, said hello, and then they were in the air.

And Dora felt no unease at all.

CHAPTER SEVENTEEN

Hawk enjoyed the flight to Washington State with Dora, the beautiful lady sitting beside him. He'd never enjoyed a flight more and his heart ached to tell her so. But he didn't. They talked about all of his travels and how he loved what he did. He realized with her sitting beside him that he was lonesome on his trips. His mind was always on his business and not where he didn't want it to go, to the loneliness that had slowly started to come on harder and harder through the years but never like now. Knowing and trying to ignore that he had no one to share his life with had never been so sharp until now.

Until meeting Dora, and now having her sitting beside him as the land below was left behind he knew that he was as happy as he'd ever been. As they flew above the clouds, her asking him questions and hearing the sound of excitement in her soft voice put hope in his heart. More like this was what he wanted.

"Maybe you'll go with me on other trips," he said, before stopping himself.

Her lips lifted and her eyes glowed. "I'm loving this trip already. But you're used to traveling alone and might get tired of me trailing along."

He hitched a brow. "I'm not a fool, having you beside me is already making this the best trip of my life." There, he'd said it and meant it.

When they landed, they got their black Jeep rental and drove to Anacortes, Washington. There they got their tickets for the ferry to San Juan Island.

When he'd driven onto the ferry and parked among the other vehicles he looked over at Dora. "Let's get out and go upstairs to the deck and enjoy the ride and the scenery."

"That sounds great. I've never been on the ferry before so it will be great to see the view."

"Let's go. You'll see the other islands as we go past.

She didn't hesitate and was out of the Jeep almost instantly. They met at the front of the Jeep and he reached for her hand as they walked toward the stairs that led up to the deck, away from the cars and she held on as they walked. Right. That was how it felt to have her by his side.

The ferry was crowded but there was plenty of space. Many rode inside, sitting at the round tavlesa. And some like them took to the top deck.

"Like I told you earlier, I've never ridden a ferry either," Dora said the moment they were standing against the railing and looking forward. "This is going to be beautiful."

He grinned. "It is. You're going to love it."

Standing there together as the ferry left the dock and started across the bays. They talked and laughed as the birds flew about them, above and dipped down to those who were tossing feed out to them. The sky was blue, and the wind rushed over them. He looked at Dora. "The wind can get crazy."

She chuckled and to his surprise, she pulled her phone from her pocket and snapped a picture of him. "What's that for?" he asked, startled that she would take his picture.

Smiling huge, she turned the phone to him and he laughed. He was looking at her in the picture with eyes of appreciation but it wasn't his expression that got the photo it was his hair standing up in a salute to the wind as it fluttered around on top of his head.

"Now that's a picture." He laughed.

"Yes, it is. I'll keep it."

He laughed. Started to calm his hair down with his hand, but he knew as he looked back out at the wind blowing in his face that it was useless. He felt the hair moving again and put his hand down, and he didn't care. Dora took his picture and was smiling. He had a hat in the Jeep and when they docked he'd put it on. But right now, knowing he'd made her smile was well worth the show his hair was putting on.

Without worrying about it anymore, he pointed out the smaller islands as they passed. "Each island has its own uniqueness. But San Juan is my favorite. Friday Harbor is a fun town to walk around in, and the island is beautiful. There are a lot of small homes, places to visit. We'll take a drive all the way around and sit on the far side facing the Canadian border, where we will probably see Orcas.

"I'd love to see them," she said, looking forward and her beautiful golden hair waved in the wind. It was too long to stand up in the wind like his but it loved to dance and he loved watching it.

"I think you will," he said, pulling his gaze off of her and back to the horizon. "We're in the right season."

"Thank you for inviting me. I'm starting to see why my sisters love to travel so much."

He grinned. "Yeah, it's cool seeing places you've never been."

And without thinking, he put his arm around her in a protective mode, putting his hand on the other side of her on the railing.

"Protecting you in case the boat jumps or something," he said as she looked up at him. They were very close.

She smiled. "Thank you for your protection, my hero."

If only, the thought ran through his brain. He wanted to say, "I'd like to be more than the hero to you. I'd like to be your husband." But he didn't.

Again, he couldn't rush these feelings he was having.

But as she continued looking up at him, he was unable not to dip his head down and kiss her. Then he looked forward and she did too, and he enjoyed riding the ferry to San Juan Islands with his arms wrapped around the woman he loved.

Yep, he knew he did. There was nothing about this woman he did not adore and love, and there was no denying it. Just the thought of her going on trips with him was like a dream he had never dreamed before. But he wanted it. And he prayed she would realize on this trip she wanted it too.

* * *

The trip was fantastic.

The meal, the first night, and walking around and watching the sunset at the winery, where their rooms were, was beautiful. His company was the best. They had dinner there and then headed to bed. Her room was first and he walked her to it, gave her a gentle kiss then headed to his room, his heart thundering for what life could be like.

The next day they went and looked at the home that he had bought and his mind and hers too went to work instantly on what could be done in the remodel. It was amazing, as usual. It had large windows, several rooms, and in his thoughts it would make a great bed and breakfast.

"Yes, it would," she said, walking down the hallway as he followed, loving watching her take in his world. "I'm sure there is a large need here," she said, spinning to look at him, he almost ran her over. His hands went to her arms and they laughed at the near collision.

"You're good at this," he said, giving her a hug.

"I see why you love it so."

He knew in that moment he'd give it all up for her. But he'd keep doing it and taking her with him... if he got what he wanted. "We better head out," he said. "I'll be coming back soon."

"I can't wait to see it finished."

He almost said work with me, but didn't. They locked up and went back to the Jeep. His mind was on the lady beside him instead of the house.

* * *

Dora's mind was on the man walking beside her from the house he was going to remodel. It was amazing how he saw things that she saw too, remodeling was like creating a bunch of sea shells and making them into a piece of art that would attract buyers best. She loved it.

She'd never thought about putting her creative mind into remodeling, until now. This property was going to be amazing. She didn't even want to ask what it was going to sell for, but she had a feeling it was probably a very large amount.

They headed to the SUV and then to the winery down the road from where they were staying. It was very beautiful. It also had a lot of lavender growing around it and other flowers. It was very nice and classy and she knew there were probably a lot of weddings that happened here.

They walked in and were led to a beautiful table set

near the edge of the patio. The breeze was blowing. Music, soft music played from a live band across the way.

"This reminds me a little bit of Hawaii, just in a different way," she said.

He smiled. "That's what I thought."

They sat down. The waitress came and Dora thought about Lettie the waitress from Hawaii. She had told Kat about her, and they were communicating. Dora didn't know yet whether she had decided to hire her, but her sister was very glad to hear about it. And she knew that if it was meant to be, it would be. They both ordered a meal of Seared Salmon, herbed pearl couscous that the waitress said the chef was amazing at creating. She was right, it was a masterpiece, the salmon superb and fresh, with handcrafted pasta. Dora was thrilled and again, Hawk had been right about his choices of everything, including the food.

As they finished the meal, he had reached out and was holding her hand because he was sitting a little closer to her because it was a stone round table and the seats were positioned so that they had a view of the gardens.

And she liked that too, maybe too much.

The night before, when they had gone up to their rooms, he had taken her into his arms and given her a gentle good-night kiss and then he had let her go and gone back to his room, and she had comfortably gone into her room. Feeling no stress that he was putting pressure on her for anything she did not want to do made her happy, she wanted the relationship to stay comfortable like it was right now. But she also felt something new that she loved. But she needed time and was thankful he didn't put her in a position where she wasn't ready to go yet. Tonight she was nervous as they stopped at her door.

"This was a wonderful day," he said then kissed her gently. "Thank you for coming with me. I'm telling you, I travel a lot, but you made this the most special trip I've ever been on."

She smiled, relaxing. "That's hard to believe, but thank you for saying that."

"No, I'm serious. I like having you with me, Dora, the truth is I haven't dated in a long time and I'm glad for that. But, when I met you, I knew that my life was changing. And it has. I'm just letting you know, upfront, that I've tried to hold back and not rush anything. But I can't help but think that there's something that's bothering you. That you're holding back from everyone. I'm here if you ever want to talk, and if I'm assuming something wrong, then I'm sorry."

She gave his hand a squeeze. "I do have something

that I've had on my mind a lot. It has nothing to do with you. It has to do with something in my past. I don't want to do it here, but when we get home, I'll tell you."

"Okay." He held her close again and kissed her gently on the lips. "Then good night. We'll leave early in the morning."

She opened her door and went inside. She leaned against the door and let emotions fight it out inside of her, but her smile won out. She would see him tomorrow and she would tell him her past. She was already ready to see him again.

She was ready to talk to him about her past, ready to take relief in telling someone, and she knew that she loved this man and he could be trusted with anything and everything.

CHAPTER EIGHTEEN

Nothing about the trip had disappointed him.

Hawk knew whatever it was she was going to tell him was something she kept private, kept deep inside, and hadn't trusted anyone with it, even her family. But she trusted him, just knowing that, filled him with hope. Hope that she had feelings for him.

When they reached his house, he gave her a hug, holding her close and taking in the moment of them being together. Then he looked into her blue eyes and kissed her again. Finally, he asked, "Do you want to meet me on the rock tonight? Our special place and if you're ready to, then tell me what you were going to tell me?"

She nodded, took a breath as if getting up courage.

Or, determination. "Yes, that will be the perfect place. I'll meet you at sunset."

"I'll be there. It was a great trip."

"Yes it was." She got into her vehicle, backed out, and headed home. He hated seeing her SUV drive down his drive then off of his land. He wanted her in this house that she was now a part of. It was their house and he wanted more than anything for her to live here with him.

Tomorrow, the roof would be finished. And there was just very little left to do, but the house had made an amazing transformation. And he wanted her in it with him. Not just in it but in his life as his wife and he knew that with everything in him.

He unpacked, busied himself with everything he needed to get done, and prepared for tomorrow. He ate a quick meal.

And then, as the sun began to go down, he walked out to the rock.

She was already there, watching the setting sun.

He took a breath, walking through the sand, not wanting to startle her. He said quietly, "It's a beautiful sunset."

She turned. "Yes, it is."

She patted the rock. He climbed up and sat down beside her.

And then she started talking. "I trust you. More than I've trusted anyone other than my family, ever. I'm gonna tell you why I'm so quiet and drawn in and don't date."

He wanted to touch her, simply place his hand on her hand, but he didn't want to do anything to take her mind off what she had to tell him. He could tell she did not like what she was about to share with him. He had a feeling he wasn't going to like it either. "I'm here for you," he said gently. "You can tell me anything and trust me."

Her gaze met his. "I know that so thank you. Several years ago I went out with this man and it changed my life. He tried to molest me. He grabbed me first in the car and tried to force me to kiss him."

The moment she said the guy grabbed her and was going to force her to kiss him Hawk's fists clenched together beside him. He had to force himself to restrain his anger as it raged through him. He kept it all to himself, knowing she needed to get this out in the open for herself.

"I bit him hard, my only defense at that moment."

Relief filled Hawk.

"Then he yanked me and I kneed him hard as he pulled me on top of him giving me the ability to use my knee for defense instead of my teeth."

The woman had the perfect response.

"He screamed, because I kneed him so hard and that gave me the moment to get away, push the door open and escape. Thank the good Lord, he gave men weak spots."

Hawk couldn't help but speak then. "Yes, He did and now I understand. I'm so thankful your knee knew where to ram."

Her lips lifted slightly at his words. "I am too."

Hawk knew how a precise hit in that spot could put a man down and he was thankful she had been able to get that done.

"The creep hadn't been able to chase me down the beach and thank God I made it out and away okay. But, I've never told this to anyone," she said quietly. "Now I'm starting to think maybe I should have so he couldn't get away with it with someone who couldn't get a shot at his weak spot."

Anger raged through Hawk, his hands clenched with the want to grab the scum bag man and hurt him. "What happened to that guy?" he asked, his voice gruff. "He needs to be taken down by the police, not your knee. Thank goodness for your sharp thinking."

She took a breath at his words and looked stronger. "I don't have to worry about him hurting anyone else, despite the fact that I worried about not having called him out. I saw in the paper a week later that he had tried it with someone else. Her scream had drawn someone from that secluded beach to come to her rescue. The man had yanked open the door, pulled the man out, held him down and called the cops. The hero was a man who had simply come out to the beach to enjoy the night. Like I do now here on my rock. Our rock."

His heart thundered at her words. Our rock.

"I'm so glad the hero was there for her. And I wish someone had been there for you."

"Thankfully the woman, like me, hadn't been harmed. The man went to jail and I don't keep up with him anymore. I think he got a great sentence because there was another one who he had harmed badly. Her family came in and heavy charges were given, life in prison because he killed her."

Hawk's heart jumped, thinking that it could've been Dora who had died.

"My heart hurts horribly, for that poor lady. I haven't put myself out there since then. I live, or had been living a quiet life since then. Just me, no dating, no putting myself out there, just enjoying my family, my ranch, my sisters, my shop and this rock. This is my safe place."

"I get it," he said, so thankful she was safe. "Who taught you to fight? Or was it just instinct? You do have great instinct."

"I read an article once about a man's weak spots and it was eyes, nose, throat and groin. I nibble my lip as you've noticed and the man was trying to force me to kiss him so that was my first instinct then the knee. I now own a gun too. Thankfully I've never used it to protect myself, but I have it. I keep it in my store, attached safely under my countertop. I don't feel unsafe anymore and I don't make the mistake of going out anymore."

His heart hurt for her but he'd known she was a small but strong woman and she was. "You are a strong woman Dora. I'm honored that you went out with me."

She smiled, her eyes glittering in the moonlight and he knew more than ever before that he loved her with all his heart.

"Until I met you, I feared that I would make a wrong decision. But Hawk," here voice trembled. "You taught me to trust you. And I trust you with everything in me."

Joy filled him that she would trust him, especially now knowing her story. He took her hands in his, there on their rock in the beautiful moonlight. "I have to tell you, I would never hurt you. I love you, Dora. I've loved you from almost the moment we first met. As I've slowly gotten to know you cautiously, because in my heart of hearts, I felt like there was something that you kept inside."

She smiled, a tender smile that cut deep into his heart even further than he knew anything ever could. "Hawk I've loved every moment I've spent with you. I couldn't believe it when you were brought to sit beside me in Hawaii. It is as if me sitting here with you now, was meant to be. And remodeling the house, has filled me with something creative I never thought about before."

He smiled. "You sweet lady have made my day, my life and there is a creative mind behind those beautiful eyes of yours that is amazing. I was thrilled you helped me remodel that house because Dora, you and only you are the reason I chose to stay here."

Her lips spread into that beautiful smile of hers and his heart thundered. "I'm glad you chose to stay."

"I am too, and I may be messing up but I can't help it… Dora, would you be my wife? Do you trust me to love you forever, to protect you, to travel with you and take you to places and enjoy life together? I'm fine. I can learn to live with it if you can't do that. But tonight, sitting on our rock after you opened your heart to me, I feel like it's the right time to ask—if it's the wrong timing I'll wait. If you don't love me I'll leave you to have the peace that I want you to have."

Her gaze drew him and he hoped with all his heart that he hadn't just made the biggest mistake of his life, asking her too soon. Asked her on the night she'd trusted him with her story. But it was done and now, he waited...

* * *

Dora's heart danced wildly inside her chest. She was cherishing the feel of his hands on hers, the strength in him, the love she saw shining, glistening in the moonlight, in those amazing eyes of his. In his eyes she saw the new world ahead of her, waking up and seeing this incredible man every morning. Tears of joy filled her eyes and certainty filled her heart.

"I would love to be your wife and live with you in that wonderful house we built together." She cried then with joy as she threw her arms around him and he drew her in, squeezed close as he kissed her and whispered, "I'll love you forever and ever, Dora. Love has everything to do with how we live this life and I want you beside me always."

She leaned back, cupped his face in her hands. "Exactly. I love that song, 'What's Love Got to Do with It' because true love, loving your family, everything is what life should be about, and finding the right love to share it with is what life is all about."

"Yes, ma'am. We are going to have a wonderful life. Love has everything to do with it."

Then she smiled. *"Everything.* So, when are we going to do this?"

He grinned. "As soon as you want."

Emotion like she'd never felt before filled her. "How about a plane ride to Vegas?"

Hawk's expression blew up into a brilliant smile. "Are you talking about marrying me right now?"

She laughed with joy. "As soon as you can get us there."

"Darl'n, it's about to happen. I'll make the call to Beck, his company flies all hours.

"Perfect," Dora said, and it was perfect as Hawk took his phone out and with one hand dialed and the other pulled her closer.

"We're about to take the ride of our dreams. I love you, Dora."

"And I love you, Hawk. So when do we fly?"

He spoke into the phone then smiled at her. "The plane will be here in an hour."

"Then, its time to pack."

He laughed drew her into his lap and leaned her back in the moonlight. "Darl'n this is going to be the trip of our life, with you sitting right here works too."

This rock is our starting point. But like you've shown me there is a whole world out there to explore beside you."

"Then let's get busy," he said and kissed her.

Dora knew for certain that she was home right here in his arms no matter where they traveled together... love had everything to do with it.

Her heart was full of love and as the kiss ended she smiled looking into Hawk's loving gaze. "I love my sisters, but now know what I want for them. I want them to one day, when the time is right for them to know what I know. What my namesake knew and I love that I know now."

Hawk's smile spread wide across his face. "And what is it that you, Melvina Eldora McConnell, soon to be Dora Harrison, know?"

She smiled, so full of love and a future of laughter and exploring with this man. "That life is full of beauty, joy, sadness and love. And loving someone who shares all of that with me is a comfort I want them to have too. I look forward to traveling down that road with you. I think they'll find that there is someone who can do the same with them."

Hawk gently brushed a hair from her cheek. "We'll enjoy watching it happen as we enjoy traveling our life together from here on out."

Her heart fluttered with anticipation. "Yes we will. Now, my life traveling Hawk, zoom in and kiss me then lets catch a flight to Vegas and make it real."

Hawk's eyes lit in the moonlight and then did exactly what she'd asked for, he swooped in, his lips joined hers and like fireworks in the moonlight they kissed.

Life was good, oh so good and Dora kissed Hawk with all of her heart. Their life was now going to be an adventure and she planned to enjoy every moment of it.

EPILOGUE

Pearl had come home the moment her job in Switzerland ended, and over a month since learning her sister, Dora, had flown to Las Vegas and gotten married! She simply couldn't believe it.

She and Kat had talked on the phone often since Dora called them from Vegas with the news and flashing a beautiful wedding ring for them to see. They'd seen the joy in her expression and heard it in her voice. And they'd seen the same in Hawk's eyes when he told them he would always put Dora first in his life that he meant it and they believed him.

Now Pearl's plane had landed and she was home, and Kat was too and in less than an hour, they were meeting at Kat's restaurant. Pearl was excited to see them.

WHAT'S LOVE GOT TO DO WITH IT

She drove from the airport to her house that sat on the bay of Star Gazer Island. Their dad and mom were out of town or they'd be throwing a big party to celebrate. But they'd already done that with Dora and Hawk, she'd just been unable to get home because of her schedule. Now she was home and more than ready to stay here for a while.

Ever since realizing her sweet sister had found love, Pearl had thought about what would it be like to find love like that? The problem, was she willing to give up her traveling schedule to find love?

Once in her garage she walked into her small home, dropped her bags off and headed straight through the house and out onto her patio. She breathed in the air as her gaze took in the view of the ocean and its open waters. This was her amazing place in the world and she smiled. Then she walked back into the house, pulled her suitcase into her room, jumped in the shower, and got ready to head to Kat's awesome restaurant.

This time they were meeting to celebrate Dora's happiness face to face and she couldn't wait to hug sweet Dora. She and Kat both knew something had bothered Dora but now she was different. She'd married and had someone to share her life with and it seemed to have eased any strain she'd felt. She'd told them that she wasn't wasting a day so that was why she was already married.

Married and happy and that made Pearl happy. And their parents. She couldn't even imagine the shock on her mom's and dad's faces when they'd gotten the call from Dora and Hawk. Yes, she'd talked to them since and they were thrilled and already talking about hopefully soon getting a grandbaby, since they had *two* married childnen now.

Pearl was smiling at the thought as she walked outside later, climbed into her SUV and headed to the Café By The Seaside, it was time to see her sisters.

When she drove up, she was thrilled to see Dora getting out of her own SUV. They both smiled and threw their arms open, actually jogged to each other and hugged.

"I am so thrilled for you, Dora."

Dora, with a smile beaming on her face, waved a beautiful ring on her finger. "I am now Mrs. Dora Harrison, and I love it because I love him. You're going to love him when you meet him too."

"I already do, saw the love in his eyes on our phone call. Come on, let's go see Kat and get this celebration started," Pearl said.

They got inside the restaurant and instantly Kat, who must have been watching for them, rushed up and engulfed them in a group hug.

"I'm so glad we're together to celebrate," Kat said

with glee and a tight hug. "Come on, the table is waiting."

They followed her through the restaurant, down the stairs, past several other tables along the stairwell area to the last one, their table. And there waiting was a bottle of champagne, it was toast time and beside it was a beautiful cake that had "Congratulations, we love you, Dora" written across it.

Cake and champagne, it was definitely a celebration.

"So we're having that first?" Pearl asked.

Kat laughed. "Yes, we are. We can eat in just a little bit. But this is for us three being here together celebrating. Our last time we were here, you and I were worried about Dora, though she didn't know it. And now she's already ran off to Vegas, of all places, and gotten married. I tell you, I just never imagined."

"Me either," Pearl said and chuckled with delight.

Dora laughed, her eyes bright. "I never thought I'd be flying anywhere, and when Hawk asked me to marry him, I couldn't wait. So off we flew. We both had been thinking about that for a little while, and yes, it was fast, and I mean, it's so unusual, but a lot of people get married that quick, you know? It's not shocking, actually."

"We're happy for you," Kat said and Pearl agreed.

Then they all sat down. Kat went to pour the glasses with the cold champagne then started slicing the cake and placed a piece on each of their plates.

Then with a smile she lifted her glass. "Cheers to a happily-ever-after for our sweet Dora. May you have a wonderful, full, and beautiful life with this handsome cowboy, the Star Gazer home builder that travels the world."

"Cheers," they said, then tapped their glasses together and took a sip. All smiling, they then set their glasses down on the table and Pearl could feel the joy between them like a huge hug.

She then laughed, couldn't help it. "Dora, when you called and told me, I was so happy. Then Kat called and told me about how many homes he remodels all over the world, I was floored. Hawaii and I think she said he had one in New Zealand that he did. I guess you're going there soon. And for your honeymoon, you went back to Kona. I won't be able to keep up with you."

Dora's eyes twinkled. "Yes, we went back to Kona, this time as a couple because that was our special place since that's where we first accidentally met up. Now, we'll be traveling a lot together. But, it's like we had a matchmaker in heaven looking down on us, you know? Of all the places that two people could travel at one time without even knowing it. Neighbors actually. It's a crazy story. Now, y'all won't be able to keep up with me. It's wonderful."

"Yes it is," Kat said, excitement in her voice.

"I love it," Pearl added and really meant it. She was drawn by the happiness in her sister's eyes and her voice. There was life there that hadn't been there before. Her shy, quiet sister beamed.

Kat smiled. "While y'all were on Kona for your official honeymoon I was actually at one of the other islands researching opening a new restaurant. I just love the islands, and who knows, one day I might make Kona my home and come visit y'all here."

Dora reached out and grabbed her hand. "I could tell you loved it and especially the fishing. You should see her there, Pearl. I mean she's vibrant now, but in Hawaii, it's like she's at peace. I mean, she just loves it. And even though we own a ranch there she doesn't visit it. Me and Hawk did on our trip and its great. You should go sometime, Kat. You don't have to ride a horse, but the cowboy who manages it is really nice."

Pearl could see that there was a difference when her sister talked about it. But there was no way Kat was moving there. And her not going to the ranch was no surprise.

"That's where Mom and Dad go when they travel to Kona and Kauai but I don't visit the ranch," Kat stated again. "I enjoy my seaside spot. But if I do relocate to Kona, we're all just a plane ride away."

Dora and Pearl smiled. Kat picked up her champagne glass and lifted it up in the air. "Here's to new horizons. Who knows? Dora, one day if I ever do find the man, yes, I might marry, I have a feeling he might be in Kona."

Pearl laughed. "Well, I have to say, I love traveling, but to me, Star Gazer Island is my home. And I love Italy, but I wouldn't live there. I could have a ton of jobs, but I came home because I wanted to see y'all, and this is just my place, my home. It's like our sweet brother, he came home and loves it, too."

Dora reached for her fork and then cut into the piece of vanilla cake. Pearl and Kat did the same. "I know this is going to taste fantastic because you made it," she said, then took the first bite. "Oh my goodness," she said, the taste so delicious.

Dora did the same. "Amazing."

"I made it just for Dora, and for us, Pearl. This is to celebrate Dora's wedding and our freedom." She grinned. "After all, Dad and Mom have two chances of getting grandbabies soon. So, *Pearl*, we can relax."

Pearl chuckled. "It's true and takes the pressure off. Thanks Dora. I'm just not ready but I love seeing you and Matt happy."

Dora nodded. "It is amazing. I'm so happy. I'm married and now a traveler and a remodeler too, and loving every minute of it."

Pearl reached around and gave her sister a hug, leaning over from her chair so they could connect. "You didn't have to change, but we like that you love it and that you have someone to do it with. Me, I don't need someone to travel with. I go and I just enjoy what I do enough to not have to worry about that. But for you, I'm thrilled. Now, let's order something other than just this amazing cake. We'll eat some dinner because I've been flying all day. After some real food is consumed, I'll finish my cake."

Dora agreed. Kat motioned and immediately food came down the steps with smiling waiters and waitresses, and their favorites were sitting before them. Pearl couldn't imagine life any better than what she had it.

And even though they hadn't mentioned Olivia this time, because she realized this wasn't Olivia's time, this was Dora's time. But as she looked at her sisters, she knew they were all at that moment thinking about their friend. And Pearl was happy. She lifted her eyes to heaven. She was happy and knew where her soul would be one day up there beside Olivia, and that made Pearl smile.

God was good and until that time came she would travel the world and use her talent to make people smile. But, for a moment as she looked at Dora's happy face she wondered what it would feel like to know the love that Olivia knew, that Matt knew and now Dora knew?

Inside something stirred and she knew one day she would be ready to explore it, but not yet. Right now, she was here, home to rest and relax on Star Gazer Island.

She would enjoy being around her family more…maybe find out at some point she was going to be an aunt. Was she ready to test the waters on settling down?

A lot of questions flooded her but she pushed them away and focused back on her sisters. This was their time and she was so glad to share this moment overlooking the ocean feeling the happiness that surrounded them. There in her mind was no other place like Star Gazer Island…she'd traveled a lot but this was home.

About the Author

Debra Clopton is a USA Today bestselling & International bestselling author who has sold over 3.5 million books. She has published over 81 books under her name and her pen name of Hope Moore.

Under both names she writes clean & wholesome and inspirational, small town romances, especially with cowboys but also loves to sweep readers away with romances set on beautiful beaches surrounded by topaz water and romantic sunsets.

Her books now sell worldwide and are regulars on the Bestseller list in the United States and around the world. Debra is a multiple award-winning author, but of all her awards, it is her reader's praise she values most. If she can make someone smile and forget their worries for a few hours (or days when binge reading one of her series) then she's done her job and her heart is happy. She really loves hearing she kept a reader from doing the dishes or sleeping!

A sixth-generation Texan, Debra lives on a ranch in Texas with her husband surrounded by cattle, deer, very busy squirrels and hole digging wild hogs. She enjoys traveling and spending time with her family.

Visit Debra's website and sign up for her newsletter for updates at: www.debraclopton.com

Check out her Facebook at:
www.facebook.com/debra.clopton.5

Follow her on Instagram at: debraclopton_author

or contact her at debraclopton@ymail.com

Made in the USA
Middletown, DE
26 June 2025